TESSA RADLEY

PRIDE &
A PREGNANCY
SECRET

Published by Silhouette Books
America's Publisher of Contemporary Romance

With heartfelt thanks to Melissa Jeglinski
for her enthusiastic support for the
DIAMONDS DOWN UNDER continuity.
Thanks also to the five authors who created this series with
me—and a special thanks to Bronwyn Jameson for generously
sharing her knowledge and experience.

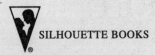 SILHOUETTE BOOKS

ISBN-13: 978-0-373-76849-3
ISBN-10:   0-373-76849-4

PRIDE & A PREGNANCY SECRET

Visit Silhouette Books at www.eHarlequin.com

Printed in U.S.A.

Books by Tessa Radley

Silhouette Desire

Black Widow Bride #1794
Rich Man's Revenge #1806
The Kyriakos Virgin Bride #1822
The Apollonides Mistress Scandal #1829
The Desert Bride of Al Zayed #1835
Pride & a Pregnancy Secret #1849

*Billionaire Heirs

TESSA RADLEY

loves traveling, reading and watching the world around her. As a teen Tessa wanted to be an intrepid foreign correspondent. But after completing a bachelor of arts and marrying her sweetheart, she became fascinated with law and ended up studying further and becoming an attorney in a city practice.

A six-month break traveling through Australia with her family re-awoke the yen to write. And life as a writer suits her perfectly; traveling and reading count as research and as for analyzing the world…well, she can think "what if" all day long. When she's not reading, traveling or thinking about writing, she's spending time with her husband, her two sons—or her zany and wonderful friends. You can contact Tessa through her Web site, www.tessaradley.com.

THE HAMMOND~BLACKSTONE FAMILY TREE

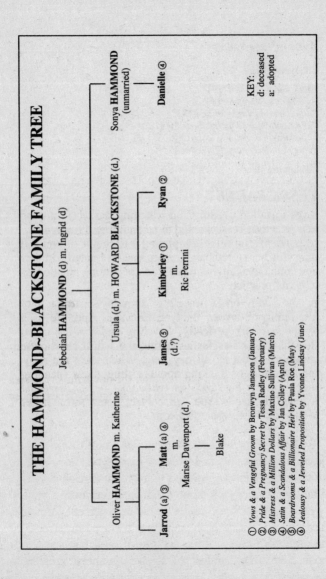

Jebediah HAMMOND (d) m. Ingrid (d)

Oliver HAMMOND m. Katherine

Ursula (d.) m. HOWARD BLACKSTONE (d.)

Sonya HAMMOND (unmarried)

Jarrod (a) ③   Matt (a) ⑥
                m.
                Marise Davenport (d.)

                Blake

James ⑤   Kimberley ①   Ryan ②
(d.?)   m.
                Ric Perrini

Danielle ④

KEY:
d: deceased
a: adopted

① *Vows & a Vengeful Groom* by Bronwyn Jameson (January)
② *Pride & a Pregnancy Secret* by Tessa Radley (February)
③ *Mistress & a Million Dollars* by Maxine Sullivan (March)
④ *Satin & a Scandalous Affair* by Jan Colley (April)
⑤ *Boardrooms & a Billionaire Heir* by Paula Roe (May)
⑥ *Jealousy & a Jeweled Proposition* by Yvonne Lindsay (June)

One

"It's time to wake, sleeping beauty." The voice was deep, dark and achingly familiar.

Jessica Cotter's eyelashes fluttered in response. A masculine hand cupped her shoulder and stroked her skin. Her lover's touch. Warm and secure under the down duvet, Jessica gave a small moan of contentment and snuggled deeper under the bedclothes.

"Wake up, Jess."

Even through the mist of sleep she sensed him coming closer, bending over her. Instead of kissing her, he pulled the covers back. Screwing her eyes tightly shut to resist the onset of the day, Jessica curled into a ball and murmured a protest.

Then she caught his scent. One hundred percent pure male. Turn-on sexy. A hint of the heat they'd shared in the dark of the night still clung to the air. The protest became a soft moan. She shifted against the sleek satin sheet, stretched a little. Her body arching toward him, her eyes still closed, she waited for his touch.

His fingers tightened on her flesh. This time he gave her shoulder a little shake.

"Get up, Jessica!"

She opened her eyes. It took a moment to get her bearings. Ryan Blackstone's penthouse.

The morning of his father's funeral.

Howard Blackstone's funeral. Little wonder Ryan wasn't in the mood for—

"Wipe that. You don't need to get up yet." He interrupted her thoughts. "I'll shower first. I need to get moving. Take your time."

Jessica sat up, wide awake now, and reached for the covers intent on hiding her suddenly inappropriate nakedness. She need not have worried. Ryan was already turning away.

She collapsed back against the pile of pillows and felt a hollow heaviness filling the pit of her stomach. The sound of the shower hissed in the bathroom. A sideways glance at the clock on the bedside table revealed that it was much later than it should be…. Damn, she'd overslept.

They both had.

The running water stopped. Jessica didn't move. She waited. The bathroom door opened and Ryan emerged, towelling his dark hair, surrounded by steam billowing out of the bathroom behind him.

He was utterly, unashamedly naked. His wide chest bare, his narrow hips lean. The most gorgeous male she'd ever known. Jessica watched furtively from under her lashes as he glanced at the Seamaster on his wrist, made an impatient sound and headed for the walk-in closet.

She closed her eyes.

God, this was going to be difficult.

"Are you asleep again?" Even with the hint of impatience, his voice was deep, a sexy rasp that never failed to ignite her senses.

Her eyelids flicked open. Immaculately dressed in a dark suit that contrasted with the crisp white cotton shirts he preferred in Sydney's February heat, he was picking his way through the clothing they'd torn off last night and dropped on the floor. Jessica felt herself flush at the memory. He must've read something in her face because his eyes darkened with secret knowledge and he came toward her. He reached the bed and bent over her, planting a muscled arm on either side of her, and his eyes softened.

"You are the most tempting woman in the world," he murmured.

He smelled clean and fresh—of soap and man. "And you're easily tempted?"

"I could stay here the whole day."

His words cast a shadow over her thoughts. So much would happen today. Howard Blackstone's funeral…the will reading…the discussion she needed to have with Ryan. Yet, despite everything hanging over her, he was irresistible.

One last kiss. That's all, she promised herself. Jessica threaded her arms around his neck and tugged.

"Hey." He landed on the bed beside her, his face so close to hers she could see the jade hue of his irises, the verdant richness that never failed to set her heart pounding. His jaw was tanned and smoothly shaven, his features strong and bold.

His hand stroked a tendril of hair out of her eyes. "You look tired. Pale. There are shadows under your eyes this morning. I shouldn't have kept you up so late."

"No problem." She forced a smile to conceal her worry about him. Their predawn lovemaking had held a certain desperation. The disappearance of his father's jet and the subsequent recovery of Howard Blackstone's body had blighted Ryan. On her part, the desperation came from other causes…a sense of time running out.

Irrevocably.

She changed the subject. "You're meeting Ric before the funeral, aren't you?"

At the mention of Ric Perrini, interim chairman of Blackstone Diamonds and his sister's husband, Ryan's mouth tightened into a hard line. "No. I'll have plenty of time to talk to him afterwards."

Jessica hesitated, then said softly, "Today is going to be hard on Kimberley as well." Ryan's sister had returned to Australia after her father's death having spent the previous ten years working for Matt Hammond, the son of Howard Blackstone's most bitter enemy—his brother-in-law, Oliver.

"I know."

Jessica almost said, "Go easy on her," but bit the words back at the last minute.

Ryan wouldn't want her counsel. She was only his lover, after all, not his wife.

Heck, she was less than his lover—she was the secret mistress that no one was supposed to know about. With a touch of dark humour Jessica wondered what people would say if they knew that the cool blonde who ran Blackstone Jewellery's Sydney store in the day came apart in the boss's arms under the dark cloak of night.

Shock. Horror. A Blackstone sleeping with a lowly member of staff? A mechanic's daughter living with a groomed-for-greatness millionaire?

A hand stroked her hair. "You know what I want more than anything in the world?"

Ryan's voice was soft, mesmerizing. For a moment Jessica

wished that the world outside these walls—the Blackstone family, Blackstone Diamonds and public expectations—could melt away. That there was only them: Jessica and Ryan. That she could curl up in his arms and never leave.

If only…

"What do you want?"

"To climb into that big bed beside you, kiss you here—" he pushed aside the cover a fraction of an inch and touched the soft skin at the base of her throat "—and celebrate life, rather than death."

He matched his actions to his words. The kiss landed on target. Jessica swallowed, her throat moving convulsively under his mouth. Then his lips moved up along her neck and landed on her mouth.

Jessica moaned.

"Open your mouth, honey, I need you."

There was a desperation she'd never heard from Ryan before. Obediently her lips parted. His mouth plundered the softness, his tongue exploring the inside of her sensitive bottom lip. Jessica moved restlessly, her arms tightening around his neck to a stranglehold. She did not want to let him go. Ryan was breathing hard when he lifted his head, and his eyes were wild.

"God, I could stay here all day. What an easy way out." His head dipped again.

The kiss was frantic and Jessica ached for him. His desire to take the easy way out, to escape, hammered home how much he dreaded the coming day. The funeral was the final proof that his father was gone. Forever. She rubbed her hands along his shoulders, wishing she could take the hurt, the pain, away from him.

He pulled back. "See how responsive your body is?" Ryan slipped a hand under the cover. "Your breasts have swollen already. I noticed last night how taut they are."

Jessica went cold.

She grabbed his wrist to stop his hand moving toward the curve of her belly. She hadn't seen any change in her body yet. Only felt the warning signs. "We haven't got time for this." Rolling away from his touch, she said, "You better get going or you'll be late."

"And you better get up, too."

"I will." She gave him a weak smile. "As soon as you're gone."

He blew out hard and raked the fingers of both hands through his hair. "I suppose it's better that way. Once you get up and start dressing I'll never get out of here. But first…"

He bent forward and placed his lips against hers for a long, lingering moment. It was a gentle kiss. Tender. A sharp contrast to the desperate passion that had gone before. "Thank you for last night."

Jessica's heart tore in half.

Ryan didn't know it yet but last night had been goodbye… although she was already wavering. Maybe another week…

He rose to his feet. A dark sombreness shadowed his eyes. "Don't be late for the funeral. And don't—"

"Don't do anything that would give us away." That hurt. Especially today. "I know."

Astonishment turned his eyes the colour of sunlight on jade. "I was about to say don't do anything that might distract me."

Her throat went dry. "Go, Ryan."

Jessica watched him stride out of the bedroom, heard his footsteps on the highly polished nyatoh wood flooring in the airy lobby. Only when she heard the elevator doors slide shut did she get out of bed.

Her stomach rolled. Bile hit the back of her throat. Jessica ran. She barely made it to the bathroom before she started retching.

Afterwards she washed her face with cold water, her hands trembling. Then she finally looked up into the mirror above the basin into her pale face with its wide-set brown eyes, the smattering of caramel freckles standing out in sharp relief. She looked absolutely ghastly. But she held her own gaze. No more pity. No more guilt. *Today*, she told herself. *You break it off today.* As soon as the funeral is over.

Before the evidence was there for everyone to see.

Ryan stood on the roughly hewn stone steps of the historic church where his father's soul was about to be rendered to immortality…or consigned to hell, depending on your view of Howard Blackstone.

There was no room for grey emotion when it came to his father, Ryan mused. You loved him…or you hated him. He had loved his father. But their relationship had not been an easy one. The midday Sydney sun beat against his back, causing sweat to bead uncomfortably inside his collar. He loosened the top button of his shirt and inhaled a deep breath.

He caught a whiff of the scent of churchyard roses. It reminded him of Jessica. The image of her spread across his bed this morning flashed through his mind. He recalled the temptation she'd offered…the desire to succumb to the passion that flared so wildly between them, and the craven impulse to push the hard reality of the day aside. He felt again his all-consuming hunger for her, for the relentless passion they shared each night that left them spent afterwards. A passion that kept him bewitched, despite that brief flare of mistrust after his father's plane went missing. A dark moment of suspicion that he'd abandoned as quickly as it had come.

From inside the church came the strains of organ music. *Abide with me*. His chest tightened.

Turning his head, Ryan glanced at the group of sombrely dressed men gathered around the hearse containing Howard Blackstone's coffin. Except for Ric, all of them would have attended his mother's funeral twenty-eight years ago. From where he stood he could see inside the hearse, could see the mahogany coffin studded with brass detail. Inside that fancy wooden box lay his father. An emotion too powerful to name choked him. His father...

"It's almost time to go in." Ric's husky voice was like a splinter of glass under his skin. Ryan spun to confront the interloper that his father had always put ahead of him, treating *him* like the eldest son.

"Give me a minute to say goodbye to my father," he snarled.

Something flashed in Ric's eyes. Ryan glared at him. The last thing in the world he wanted was Ric Perrini's sympathy. Instantly the emotion vanished and Ric's eyes returned to their usual unreadable expression.

Ryan swung away. The organ music grew louder, spilling out the open church doors. Ryan inclined his head and murmured a silent prayer. With his *Amen* ringing in his head, he brushed past Ric and headed for the rear of the hearse.

Ric's hand came down on his shoulder. "I need a quick word with you."

Ryan stiffened and he hesitated for a moment before giving a curt nod. "Sure."

They walked a short distance away and stopped beside a tall yew hedge. The sun fell across Ric's face, highlighting the shadows beneath the very direct blue eyes. "First off, you need to know that no one here today is sorrier about the loss you've suffered than I."

Ryan wondered whether the bulk of Ric's sorrow came from the rumour that his father had changed his will shortly before his death. Under the original will Ric—rather than Howard's own children—stood to inherit the majority of Howard's shareholding. Was Ric fazed by the possibility of coming into less shares now? By the possibility of Kimberley failing to inherit any shares at all?

Ryan narrowed his gaze and tried to read Ric's expression as he said, "Garth told Kim that Howard changed his will." Garth Buick, one of Howard's oldest friends and the company secretary of Blackstone Diamonds was a trustworthy source.

Ric's eyes grew shadowed. "He's warned Kim not to expect too much. Not after her defection to the House of Hammond."

From personal experience Ryan had a pretty good idea of how badly their father would've reacted. Ten years ago Ric had been appointed head of the new Blackstone retail division, making Ric second in power only to his father. Ryan had resigned from Blackstone's to go work for De Beers in South Africa. He'd needed the time away from Ric, from Howard and from Blackstone's. Howard had been madder than a riled copperhead snake at what he'd termed "Ryan's desertion."

When Ryan had eventually returned, older and wiser, his father had welcomed him back with a coolness that warned him that his desertion had not been forgotten—or forgiven—even though he'd been appointed head of Blackstone Jewellery, the retail arm of Blackstone's. The past had always lain between them, a chasm too vast to bridge. Until Ryan had taken steps to close it and told his father two weeks before Christmas that he wanted a bigger say in the company. Howard had seemed satisfied.

If Howard had changed his will back in December, it was very likely that his own share had increased—at Ric's expense.

It would not make the already strained relationship between himself and Ric any better. But inheriting the additional shares would certainly send out a message about his father's confidence in him, and put him in a much stronger position to be voted chairman of the board at the Blackstone Diamonds board meeting next Monday morning.

Pushing his thoughts aside, he came back to the puzzle posed by the new will. "But surely Kimberley will still get Mother's jewellery and a sizeable number of shares? Dad would never strip her of those." Those shares had given Ryan a few sleepless nights. Together Kimberley and Ric would hold a formidable block of stock…and votes. Who became chairman of Blackstones, he or Ryan, might depend on whether Kim inherited any shares—and on how she voted them.

"We'll know soon enough." Ric was frowning. He glanced in the direction of the church doors, then back at Ryan. "Kim thinks Matt Hammond will be in there. You and I have had our differences, but it's important we present a united front today."

Ryan stared at Ric. Since his sister had come back to Australia, she'd taken charge of public relations at the company. She'd had her work cut out controlling the fallout that had followed the downing of the chartered jet with their father—and Marise Davenport, the woman reputed to be his latest mistress—on board. With her bereaved husband, Matt Hammond, buying Blackstone Diamonds stock and triggering dangerous rumours of a takeover, the newspapers would soon be sniffing around for any signs of cracks within the company management.

Slowly Ryan nodded. "Yes, Matt Hammond will be in there, gloating in the front row. He's been telling every reporter who cares to listen that he'd be here today 'to make

ure the bastard's buried'." Ryan knew his father had many
nemies. But it rankled that Matt, the son of his mother's only
rother, shared the view. And publicly, as front page news, at
hat.

Matt Hammond was a traitorous bastard—no different from
is father, Oliver. And now he'd all but declared war on the
Blackstones. If war was what Matt wanted, that's what he'd
et.

Turning away, Ryan headed for the hearse, and rapped
ut, "Okay, time to go."

The coffin rolled out of the back of the hearse. The funeral
director, ridiculously attired in cutaway black tails and a top
at, placed atop the coffin the floral arrangement that Kim-
erley had ordered. Pure white lilies and snowy freesias. His
mother's favourites, his Aunt Sonya had said, because
Howard had always sent them to her to celebrate special oc-
asions. As the coffin slid past him, Ryan caught a hint of the
ragrance and for a sharp instant a memory of sunshine and
aughter sliced through his mind…of a time long ago, when
here had still been happiness in the Blackstone home.

And then the image was gone and reality bit in. What was
eft of his father lay under that pile of blooms, pulled out of the
plane wreckage that had been recovered a few weeks ago. It was
ard to believe he'd never hear that gruff voice again. Never have
he chance to prove to his father that he could run Blackstone's
with the same expertise and energy that Howard Blackstone had.

The six pallbearers took up their positions. Ryan was up
ront, Ric on the opposite side. Garth Buick fell in behind Ric,
while Kane, a Blackstone cousin, stood behind Ryan.
Bringing up the rear were Howard's two older brothers—
Kane's father, Vincent and William Blackstone.

Ryan's mouth tightened at the sight of William Black-
tone. Two months ago his uncle had sold his ten-per-cent

holding in Blackstone Diamonds to Matt Hammond—and se
a chain of events in motion that were currently causing havo
at head office.

Ryan bent to pick up the handle nearest him. "Right, let's go.

They hoisted the coffin up. He met Ric's level gaze ove
the top of the mahogany and fought not to let his turmoi
show. More than anything in the world he wanted to prov
that he could do the job he'd been denied during his father'
lifetime—that of chairman of Blackstone Diamonds.

The music rose to a crescendo as they entered the churcl
and the coffin handle rested heavily in Ryan's hand. A quicl
glance in the direction of the front pew failed to reveal Mat
Hammond. Surreptitiously, Ryan scanned the mourners fo
Jessica's pale hair, but failed to find it. She'd be here some
where. For a brief moment he thought about the passio
they'd shared last night, the kiss this morning, and he fel
himself relax. Jessica's generosity as a lover, the comfor
she'd so wordlessly given him, had made the day bearable.

They set the coffin down beneath the pulpit, where the
priest waited to start to the service. Kimberley beckoned from
the front row, and Ric and Ryan filed into the pew.

Once seated beside Kimberley, with Ric on her other side
Ryan took another look around. No sign of Matt Hammond
Nor Jessica.

"She's right at the back," Kim whispered.

Ryan frowned at his sister. "Who is?"

"Jessica." Kim raised an eyebrow. "That's who you'r
looking for, right?"

Ryan didn't answer.

Nor did he glance back to confirm his canny sister's sus
picions. Instead he fixed his gaze on the lonely coffin in the
front of the church and almost sighed with relief when the
priest started to speak, sparing him the need to answer.

As he listened to the priest, Ryan couldn't help wondering how Kimberley had known. She'd had always been good at reading people, but Ryan had thought he'd done a great job of hiding his affair with Jessica. So how the hell had Kim gotten wind of it?

No one knew.

He'd made sure of that.

The heat in the packed church pressed in on Jessica and the priest's voice started to fade. She squeezed her eyes shut against the wave of nausea that swept through her and by sheer will-power kept down the meagre slice of toast she'd eaten earlier.

"Honey, are you all right?" Her mother's whisper pierced her misery.

"Yes." Another wave of nausea hit. "Maybe not," she muttered through gritted teeth. Her mother didn't know about the baby…and Howard Blackstone's funeral was the last place she'd pick to make that announcement.

Morning sickness. What a misnomer. It was already noon. All-day sickness would be more accurate.

"Come, let me help you out."

"Out?" Her eyes flew open and she stared at her mother in disbelief. "You mean *leave* Howard Blackstone's funeral?" That thought was enough to make her feel ill all over again. She'd sat with her parents in the farthest back corner to avoid attracting attention. That was hard enough given her father's wheelchair. Leaving now would undo all that.

Her mother nodded. "You need to get some air. You're as white as a sheet, Jessica."

A woman with a black hat that resembled an upside-down flowerpot turned and glared at them. Jessica gave her a weak smile. Placing her hand on her mother's, she mouthed, "I'll be fine." Right.

Sally Cotter didn't look convinced. "If you say so."

The black flowerpot turned and glared again.

Jessica closed her eyes and admitted to herself that she felt dreadful. Relief swirled through her when the congregation rose and started to sing the final hymn.

"I'll see you outside." She slipped past her father's wheel-chair, making for the door. Outside she gasped in a lungful of fresh air. Moments later she stood in the restroom. After splashing water over her face, she felt cooler and a little better.

Her doctor had given her a prescription for morning sick-ness, but she'd been reluctant to take the pills. Instead she'd nearly been physically ill in the midst of Howard Black-stone's funeral. Jessica shuddered. What would Ryan have said? What rumours would have flown around? It didn't bear thinking about. Quickly she opened her bag, found the box and broke the seal, then swallowed down a tablet.

Closing the door behind her, Jessica came around the corner and saw that service was over. The mourners were spilling out the church, down the stone stairs. The sun was bright and in the hedges she could see blackbirds hopping about. The drained, ill feeling receded. She looked around for her parents but couldn't locate them. They must still be inside. She started up the stairs.

Before she could sidle through the press of people, Ryan reached her. "Jessica, I didn't see you in there. Surely you didn't stay outside?"

"I sneaked out just as the service ended, I needed the bath-room."

"Thank you for being there." There was an unaccustomed fervour in the eyes that scanned her features.

"How could I not? He was your father."

"And your boss."

"No, you're my boss," she said lightly, peering up at him through her lashes.

"Don't look at me like that!" Tension invaded his features and his eyes turned molten. "It's hard to believe, but I want you. Right now."

"Ryan!" Excitement stirred inside her, a world apart from the awful nausea that had hit her less than ten minutes ago. "What would people say?"

"Right now I don't particularly care." He caught her arm. "Jess—"

"Careful." She pulled free of his grasp. "People will talk. Believe me, later you *will* care."

Before he could reply she took off up the stairs and disappeared into the crowd, her heart beating at Ryan's unexpected intensity.

Ryan nosed the sleek black BMW M6 through the Victoria Street gate into Rookwood Cemetery and followed the hearse as it crawled along a winding lane past lines of graves. Turning into the older burial section Ryan drove slowly beside the Serpentine Canal edged with lush plantings of agapanthus, before pulling the BMW in behind where the dark hearse had stopped.

Swiftly alighting, Ryan made his way to the raw gash in the ground where a fresh grave yawned near a Norfolk pine. He set his expression, determined not to show what this day was costing him.

Ryan's stride hesitated as he glimpsed his grandfather Jeb's grave, just beyond his mother's. Beside him, his aunt Sonya paused at Ursula Blackstone's—her sister's—grave. Ryan put his arm under his aunt's elbow. She gave a start, and he patted her arm, at a total loss for words.

"I sometimes come to tend the rosebushes that Ursula planted for James. She used to visit every Sunday afternoon to tend them. I'm lucky to get here once every couple of months." Sonya's voice was thin. "Now Howard has joined them, too."

The plaque beside his mother's grave, flanked by Remember Me rosebushes, read *In memory of our missing son, James, we will see you one day.* Howard Blackstone hadn't even allowed his wife to reserve a piece of cemetery for James—the plaque was all Ursula Blackstone had to remember her son by. A tragic reminder that his parents had never seen their first-born son after the day he'd been kidnapped.

"Perhaps now the three of them are reunited." Sonya followed his gaze.

"Maybe." Ryan thought about his father's stubborn refusal to accept that James was dead. Howard had retained investigators for decades to chase a stone-cold trail. Maybe Sonya was right. In death they might all find peace.

But one thing was for certain, Ryan wouldn't need to plant rosebushes to remember his father. Howard Blackstone's strength and drive and determination were branded into him. His unspoken legacy.

They strode to the edge of the open grave prepared for his father, and Sonya started to cry in earnest. Awkwardly Ryan put his arm around his aunt and looked wildly around for his sister. Instead of seeing Kimberley, he found himself staring into the angry eyes of Matt Hammond.

From across the open grave Matt's lips moved. "I'll show you you can't mess with my family and get away with it." The words carried on the wind to where Ryan stood.

Ryan speared the other man with a furious gaze, tension coiling through him until he felt he might snap. Somewhere in the thicket of trees a kookaburra cackled. Damn bird!

Beside him, Sonya shifted restlessly. Ryan tightened his hold on her arm and she stilled.

The priest started to speak. Ryan closed his eyes for the reading and tried to absorb the solemn rhythm of the words. Then, without knowing how it happened, he was holding a fistful of earth. Stepping forward, he parted his fingers letting the red earth slip through his fingers onto the coffin.

Dust to dust.

The surge of emotion took him by surprise. His throat tightened, hot. Someone grabbed his hand. *Kimberley.* He jerked and swung away from the grave.

"Are you okay?"

He nodded, breaking free and blindly pushing through the press of the crowd, intent on getting to the back where no one would be watching. Where he could grieve in peace.

Jessica.

Had she come? He scanned the mourners. His gaze came to rest on her slim figure, her pale hair drawn off her delicate features. She wasn't standing alone as he'd half expected, a fish out of water at Howard Blackstone's funeral. Nor was she grouped with the Blackstone employees. Instead she stood a distance away with an older couple. A man in a wheelchair and a woman who on second glance looked vaguely familiar.

His attention returned to Jessica, devouring her, wishing they were a lifetime away from the cemetery and the sad memories it held. She lifted her hand in a little wave.

Ryan gave a brief nod in response and, feeling oddly comforted, turned his attention back to the grave for the final prayer. When he opened his eyes, it was to see Jessica pushing the wheelchair toward a row of parked cars.

She was leaving.

Ryan strode after her. "Jessica," he called once he was clear of the crowd. But she didn't hear and helped the man into an unfamiliar car. Ryan started to sprint. He reached her as she was about to climb into the driver's seat. It certainly wasn't Jessica's Toyota. She didn't respond to his questioning glance at the car, so he simply said, "You'll come to back to the house?"

Her brown eyes were evasive. "I've never been. So I don't think so." She glanced at the couple in the car. "I need to get my parents home."

Her parents? "Introduce us," Ryan demanded, ducking his head down to stare into the car.

"Mum, Dad, this is Ryan Blackstone," she said with a reluctance that unaccountably annoyed Ryan. With the amount of press coverage he and Kimberley had gotten in the past month, her parents would've known at a glance who he was. He supposed he should be grateful that she hadn't introduced him as her lover.

"My parents, Sally and Peter."

Her mother gave him a sweet smile. But her father's eyes were more critical. He wondered what had happened to put her father in a wheelchair. And then he wondered whether her parents knew he was their daughter's lover. Hell, he'd never thought of what she might've told them about her private life. Never considered that she might have to lie to the people she loved.

Her parents. Her friends.

A rush of shame surged through him. With his insistence on secrecy, he'd made things very awkward for Jessica. And why? Because he didn't want it to be public knowledge that he was sleeping with a member of his staff. Had be been grossly unfair to Jessica?

Stepping away from the car, he drew Jessica with him. In the distance the kookaburra laughed again. "Please come to the house, to Miramare, Jess."

"I don't think—"

For a brief moment he felt a strange sense of being abandoned. "I want you to come."

Her head jerked up at the suppressed urgency in his voice, her eyes widening. He read confusion, turmoil…and something else in the caramel depths.

"You've never invited me there before. So why now? I doubt the rest of the staff will be there."

He had no answer for that. At least not one that he understood himself. All he knew was that he wanted to be able to look across the room, and see her slim figure, hear her calming voice.

She was still waiting for an answer. Dropping his voice, he said, "I haven't mentioned it before, but there's talk that my father's changed his will…."

She must have seen something of his turmoil and anger in his eyes because after a brief pause, she nodded.

"I must see my parents home first."

"Jessica," her mother interceded, poking her head out the window. "Let's go past the Blackstone mansion. I can drive home from there."

"I don't want you driving, Mum. Not today." Jessica exchanged a long look with her mother that had Ryan feeling like he'd missed something vital. "I can call a cab to take me after I've dropped you and Dad off. And I'll catch another cab home later."

"All the way to that lonely apartment of yours in Chippendale?"

"I'll take you…home…later," Ryan added quickly. If her parents thought she was still living in the apartment she'd rented in Chippendale after moving to Sydney, that must mean that after almost a year her parents still didn't know she'd moved in to his penthouse. What had it taken for her to maintain that deception? Both of them only used cell phones, and there was no landline in the penthouse. Yet he knew Jessica visited her parents at their home on the outskirts of Sydney every weekend—without him. But he'd never thought how hard it must be to keep her mother from visiting her in return.

"That's sorted. I'll see you later." Ryan stepped away from the car with a feeling that he'd just averted a major crisis that he hadn't seen coming.

Two

Ryan barged out his father's study, past Garth Buick's outstretched hand, and strode blindly down the corridor, feeling like the bottom had just dropped out of his world. Ahead of him he could see Matt Hammond walking with long angry strides toward the front door—showing no intention of staying for refreshments.

"Ryan." At the sound of his sister's voice the sinking feeling in his stomach intensified.

Kim was whiter than the lilies that had rested on his father's coffin, her eyes glassy with shock. For the first time in years he reached for her, his own hands shaking. She was as stiff as a board in his arms. Ryan drew her into the music room next door, out of sight of curious eyes, and kicked the door shut.

"The old bastard," Ryan said bitterly.

"How could he do it? How could he disinherit me?"

Kim's voice was muffled against his suit lapel. "I'm his daughter, damn him."

"He left your shareholding in the company to someone who doesn't even exist. James is dead." Above her dark head, Ryan shook his head at the craziness of it all. Except Howard Blackstone had never been the tiniest bit insane.

A coldhearted bastard, sure.

Manipulative, yes.

But not crazy.

Except in one respect—his dogged belief that his first-born son was still alive. Somewhere.

"There's no way James is going to magically come back to life in the next six months to claim the shares—or Miramare." Ryan tried to comfort Kimberley and thought he might be making headway when she relaxed a little in his arms. James's ghost had haunted the mansion since his disappearance as a toddler. Perhaps it was fitting that his father had left Miramare to his dead brother.

"Even if he doesn't, the shares left to him will be divided between you and Ric." Kimberley sounded bereft. "I get nothing—except that cold, clear clause that he intentionally disinherited me."

Which meant he and Ric would still have an equal shareholding. Right until the end, his father was pitting them against each other.

"Dad had no right to leave Mother's jewellery to Marise Davenport." A picture of the vampish Marise flashed through Ryan's head. A flamboyant redhead, Marise had worked for Blackstones in the marketing department. He'd never paid her much attention, even though she'd tried to snare his interest often enough. It clearly hadn't stopped her. She'd snared a bigger fish. His father. In addition to his mother's jewellery she'd gotten a seven-figure cash bequest as well. Not that it did her much good now that she was dead.

And his sister had inherited nothing.

"I'm going to challenge the will." Kimberley's voice was harder than the scintillating diamond she wore on her ring finger. Ryan had never heard her use that tone before. "All my life I've been trying to get him to recognize my worth. I'm not letting him get away with it."

"It won't be easy." Neither of them had heard the door open. Ric filled the doorway. "His will states clearly that he intended to disinherit you—that was his dying wish."

Kim tugged free of Ryan's arms and rushed to her husband, "Oh, Ric, he couldn't have chosen a better way to hurt me."

"Shh, love. He's gone. Your father can only hurt you if you allow him to. You make your own happiness." Ric bent his head and placed a loving kiss on Kimberley's lips.

And suddenly Ryan felt like an intruder, an outsider to the tightly bound unit of two that his sister and Ric created. Feeling utterly alone he stepped past them into the corridor outside.

Men in suits stood in huddled clusters in the entrance hall at the foot of the double stairway, with its ornate filigree balustrade, discussing the shocking contents of the will. They grew quiet as he approached, their eyes curious. Ryan shook hands with a couple who offered condolences on the loss of his father as he passed.

The only good thing to come out the will reading was the evidence that his father had viewed him equal to Ric. But Ryan had never been able to fill the void that James's loss had created.

The emptiness within him expanded. He changed direction and headed for the grand salon, where the majority of the mourners had congregated. As he entered, the rich fragrance of fine coffee hung in the air. The sound of chatter was almost overwhelming. Had Jessica arrived yet? He searched the throng, until his gaze rested on a familiar fair head. As if drawn by his gaze, Jessica turned, her caramel-brown eyes filled with concern as they met his.

And for the first time since the funeral, the hollow feeling in his chest started to recede.

Jessica's heart softened as she took in Ryan's tight, strained expression. This last month had been hard on him. At least with the funeral and the will reading behind him, his life should regain some balance. Then she remembered his comment about a new will.

Perhaps not.

Certainly the Ryan crossing toward her was far from settled. His eyes were stormy, his jaw hard and set. Apprehension sank like a stone in her stomach. When he reached her side, she turned to him and murmured, "So the rumour was correct, Howard changed his will?"

"Yes." His voice was harsh. He pushed his hands through his groomed black hair. "Kim's been disinherited."

"Oh, no." Jessica put her hand over her mouth to stifle her gasp of horror. She'd heard there'd been some friction between Kim and her father. But her concern about Ryan subsided a little. "But you're okay?"

The look he gave her held rage and pain. "My father has left thirty per cent of his shareholding to my brother."

"Your brother?" Jessica blinked, trying to work that out. "But your brother—"

"Is dead!" Ryan cut across her. "Only my father never accepted that. He never gave up the hope of one day finding James."

Jessica's breath caught in her throat. *"He found him?"*

"No." Ryan's face darkened. "But according to Garth, Dad

was jubilant before his death. He thought he had a lead."
Ryan shook his head. "James disappeared thirty-two years
ago. I find it hard to swallow that my hard-headed father was
being led on a wild-goose chase by some two-bit charlatan."

Jessica's heart ached for Ryan. She moved a little closer
and wished they were alone, so that she could put her arms
around him and give him the hug he needed right now, even
though she suspected he'd push her away if she tried to hold
him close. He'd shut himself off. And she took care not to
touch him, not to do anything that might compromise the
understanding they'd always shared.

No one must know that they were lovers.

Not even today.

Yet she couldn't help feeling an unexpected surge of sympathy for Howard Blackstone, a man she'd always silently
despised. How terrible to have lost a child…to never be able
to bury his remains and say goodbye.

The thought of losing her unborn baby already filled her
with anguish. *How had Howard and Ursula coped?* "So what
happens now? If there's no brother to actually inherit, who
will inherit your dead brother's share?"

Ryan gave a laugh that held no humour. "In six months' time
it will revert to me and Ric in equal shares. That's in addition
to the thirty per cent we each inherited under the new will."

"Then that will be the end of it, won't it?" Jessica stared up
into the handsome features she'd come to love so much. The
jade eyes, the strong nose and beautifully moulded mouth…

A mouth that tightened into a hard line, lending a tough-
ness to Ryan's almost-perfect face. "I don't think it will ever
end. When James died my family fell apart. He was the first-
born son. The heir."

Understanding dawned. "So you tried to take his place? To
be the son your father wanted?"

He gave her a slanted look. "I'll never be that. And I wasn't alone in trying to please my father. Kim worked hard, too. Both of us excelled at school. I made the cricket and rugby teams and I competed in triathlons. I did everything I could to—" He broke off and looked away. He gave a sigh. "What does it matter? My father is dead."

And Ryan felt as if he'd never lived up to his father's expectations, Jessica concluded. It gave her insight into the man whose secret mistress she'd been for the past two years, showed her a glimpse of his character that he'd always kept firmly hidden. A part that she probably would never have discovered if it hadn't been for the new will.

Was this the real reason he held her at an emotional distance? Did he feel he was incapable of being loved?

"But at least my father didn't leave the lion's share to Ric," he said with a hint of satisfaction.

Jessica drew away. The intense rivalry between the two men—and the manner in which it consumed Ryan—had always concerned her. "Now that your father's gone, you and Kim and Ric will have the task of steering Blackstone's—"

"Ric's not a Blackstone. I'm the only surviving son. Under my leadership the profits on the retail side of the business have grown enormously. I've proved myself. Control of the board should be mine."

Jessica started to speak, chilled by the inflexibility Ryan had revealed, then bit the words back. What would be the point? Ryan had never listened to her. And from his set expression he wasn't about to start now.

Jessica took a tentative bite of a shortbread biscuit she'd taken off a passing waiter's tray. Nothing untoward occurred. Her stomach didn't heave. So she took another cautious bite.

Ryan had left a couple of minutes ago with Garth Buick

and now stood across the room with a group of dark-suited men, all wearing sombre expressions. No doubt he didn't want to be seen overlong in her company—in case it drew unwelcome speculation and more gossip.

But the attempt to wind herself up about his secrecy fell flat. The conviction that she needed to end her relationship with Ryan tonight was starting to waver. It had been such a terrible day for him, especially with what he'd told her about his brother's death.

Perhaps she should delay for another week. After all, she'd originally intended to break it off with him after the New Year, when she'd first discovered that she was pregnant. She'd already delayed once, because his father's jet had gone down—why not again? What would it really matter? Ryan spent so much time at work, so little time home, that he was unlikely to notice the changes to her routines and her body.

She turned away, determined not to give anyone a reason to suspect her connection with Ryan. A little distance away, Jessica saw Dani Hammond, Ryan's cousin and an up-and-coming jewellery designer. Her work would be featured in the launch of the new season's Something Old, Something New jewellery collection amidst much fanfare at the end of the month. The funeral of the young woman's uncle was hardly the time to go and introduce herself as a business associate, Jessica decided.

She started at the touch on her arm.

"Jess?"

Jessica turned to find Briana Davenport, one of Australia's most popular supermodels and the "face" of Blackstone Diamonds beside her. Briana's sister Marise had died in the plane crash with Howard Blackstone, along with the pilot, copilot, cabin attendant and Howard's lawyer, Ian Van Dyke. A terrible tragedy. And today Briana looked nothing like the smiling, glamorous figure who adorned billboards and double-page spreads in *Vogue Australia*. Although she wore a beautifully cut black dress that screamed couture, she looked pale and tired, her eyes red from crying, and her glorious golden-brown hair pulled back from her face into a tight knot.

"Sweetie, how are you holding up?" Jessica asked. Briana was as good a friend as any that Jessica had made since moving to Sydney. They'd met through work and the friendship had grown. Because of Briana's hectic modelling schedule they didn't see each other often—which, given her peculiar arrangement with Ryan, suited Jessica to perfection.

Briana gave a wan smile. "Two funerals in less than a month is tough to deal with. Even though Marise and I weren't close, I find myself crying at the oddest times."

"That's understandable. Don't be too hard on yourself." Jessica touched the other woman's arm. Fortunately Briana didn't know—few did—that *she* was supposed to have been on that plane with Howard. *She* should have died, too. *She* should've been buried, instead of standing here patting Briana's arm like a fraud. Jessica shivered.

She had been lucky….

If it hadn't been for Howard's obnoxiousness, she would've been dead. She'd never thought that she'd be grateful for that.

"You know what the worst of it is?"

Briana's words brought her back to the present. "What?"

"People are saying that Marise was Howard's mistress. I mean that's disgusting…he's more than thirty years older than her." Briana sniffed and fresh tears glimmered in her eyes.

"Ignore it." Jessica advised, deciding not to upset Briana further by commenting on Howard Blackstone's well-known appreciation for younger women in recent years. "It will pass. The media will soon find a new scandal—and then they'll leave the Blackstones alone. There are no hard facts to sustain that scurrilous rumour."

Briana gave her a strange look. "Haven't you heard?"

"Heard what?"

"At the will reading—"

"What about the will reading?"

"Marise inherited an astronomical sum of money under the will."

Ryan hadn't mentioned that. Jessica thought about how she'd had to drag every morsel of information out of him. Wasn't she important enough for him to share the crises that were happening in his life?

It underlined that breaking off with him was the right decision. Their relationship had no future. She had to end it, quickly.

"Marise also got Ursula's jewellery collection. Of course it means nothing now that she's dead." Briana's eyes grew dark with pain.

Poor Kimberley! Her mother's jewels had gone to a stranger. "No, I hadn't heard about that."

"And Marise's son, Blake, inherited a trust fund. People are already speculating that my nephew is Howard Blackstone's illegitimate son."

"Oh, my goodness! If that's true, Matt Hammond is really going to hate the Blackstones now. That would make the boy Ryan's—"

"Baby brother." Briana nodded. "It's terrible. The papers are going to have a field day with it once they find out."

"Oh, no." Jessica knew Briana was right. This would not give the Blackstones the privacy they badly needed in their time of grief. "Poor Kimberley. Poor Ryan. And poor Matt

Hammond." Jessica's soft heart melted for Matt. If Marise had cheated on him with Howard, and he saw Kimberley's return to Blackstone's as Howard's daughter abandoning her job with the House of Hammond, was it any wonder that the man was bitter? She could certainly understand Matt's statements to the papers that he wanted to be here today to see Howard buried. In his position, she'd have wanted to see Howard buried alive!

Briana wiped her eyes. "Shh, Ryan's coming over to say hello." She forced a small smile and held her face up for a brief, social kiss. "I'm so sorry about your father."

"Thank you." Ryan didn't glance at Jessica. "Can I get either of you ladies a drink? Coffee? There's even champagne—some people are celebrating my father's passing," he said darkly.

"I need something strong," Briana muttered. "Help me drown my sorrows." Then an expression of horror crossed her face. "Ryan, that was awful. I didn't mean it the way it came out."

"I know you didn't." He patted her shoulder. "Everyone is walking on eggshells around me right now, it's a relief to hear something that comes out wrong. Why don't you join me with a small sherry?"

"Thanks." Briana gave a sigh of relief. "I think I will."

"Jessica?" At last he looked at her and smiled politely. "What would you like?"

"I'll have a cup of tea, thanks." Her smile was equally polite, but inside she was smouldering at his cool distance, the civil facade that gave away nothing about the passion they shared every night after work.

"Tea? In this heat? Are you certain?"

She nodded. "Perfectly." She bit back her comment that he knew exactly how she liked it. "White with no sugar."

Both women watched him weave his way through the crowd

in search of a waiter. "He's such a handsome man," Briana said. "I can't believe he isn't married or at least attached."

Jessica couldn't help wishing that Briana knew about her and Ryan. But Ryan had been adamant that their affair should remain secret. Which meant that from time to time this happened: the idle speculation about Ryan's good looks, his girlfriends, his prowess in bed. It never failed to sear her with jealousy. It was when she most wanted to wring Ryan's wretched neck for putting her in this predicament. But she'd been so blinded by the stars in her eyes that she'd agreed to the arrangement. So she did what she always did at such times, she tried distraction. "Does Blake resemble Howard in any way?"

Briana's eyes widened in dismay. "Jess, don't tell me you think—"

"I don't know what I think." Jessica decided honesty was the best tactic. "But a lot of people are going to be searching for a resemblance. So you might as well think about whether there are any for them to spot."

A frown creased Briana's forehead. "I'm not sure. Blake does have dark hair…and the cutest smile. I'll have to take a look at the photos at home. I don't see him very often, with him living in Auckland and all the time I spend overseas on assignment. Poor mite. He won't have a mother. But maybe I can still play some role in his life. I'll have to speak to Matt about visiting more often."

"I'm sure Matt would appreciate your help." But Jessica couldn't help thinking of Ryan. If the rumour proved true, how would the existence of yet another brother affect him? Blake was a child. But he was a child under the guardianship of Matt Hammond. A man who had made it clear that he was out to destroy the Blackstones.

A waiter arrived and Briana helped herself to the dainty glass of sherry, then he handed Jessica a cup of tea.

"Look." Briana tilted her head in the direction of a trio of women who kept snatching avid glances in their direction and then leaning forward to whisper to each other. "They're talking about me. About Marise. I hate this."

Jessica threw the women a hard look. They had the grace to look discomfited and turn away. "Maybe they're just admiring you, sweetie."

"No, I heard them say Marise's name." Briana sounded quite upset. She set the sherry down on a table behind them. Jessica followed suit and the teacup clattered against the saucer.

"Gossips!" Jessica glared after them. "Don't they realize she's your sister?"

"We were never as close as I would've liked," Briana confided.

Jessica didn't know Marise. She'd been working in Melbourne and later Adelaide, while Marise had worked in the Pitt Street head office in Sydney. But the office chatter had been that Marise was a man-eater. Not long afterwards she'd married Matt Hammond and then Blake had been born. The gossips had speculated that she'd trapped Matt into marriage by getting pregnant.

Jessica shuddered at the thought and touched her stomach. What kind of marriage would that create? Perhaps Marise had outsmarted Matt. Perhaps she'd already been carrying Howard's child. What kind of woman would do that?

Only a very conniving kind of woman.

The kind of woman that a sweetie like Briana would've found it difficult to relate to. "Maybe Marise wasn't a woman's woman."

"She wasn't a sister's sister, either. I never really understood her." Briana looked around and lowered her voice. "A while back, when she was here for Mum's funeral, she asked to leave something in the safe in my apartment. I said yes. I looked inside the other day, and I discovered she'd left some stones."

"What kind of stones?"

"I don't know. Pink stones. I told Matt I'd found some of Marise's jewellery. He said I should keep it. But how can I do that, Jess?" Briana looked troubled. "I mean, if Matt doesn't want them, they really should go to Blake. They might even be valuable. What if they're diamonds?"

Jessica frowned. "Why don't you get someone to appraise them? There are a couple of people I use." The group in front of them shifted and through the gap Jessica could see Ryan talking to his sister, their dark heads close together. "Quinn Everard is very knowledgeable and has a great reputation, but he's a busy man. Stan Brownlee over in Manly is very good, too."

"I'll call you at the store later this week for their contact numbers," Briana murmured.

"Sure." Jessica was still watching Ryan. Even from here she could see his concern and affection for his sister in every line of his body. How she craved the same for herself. Although he cosseted her, and spoiled her with gifts and jewellery, Jessica had never felt as though Ryan *needed* her. She'd always been highly conscious that he was a Blackstone…and she was nothing more than his mistress.

"You could do a lot worse than Jessica. She's very nice."

Ryan froze. He'd ignored his sister's earlier comment in the church, hoping it was nothing more than a wild guess. But she'd never been the type to let up. And if she found out about his affair with Jessica, that would make his opposition to her relationship with Ric years ago on the basis that they worked together seem very odd.

But how was he supposed to explain that what he had

with Jessica had just…combusted? He'd never meant for it to happen. Hell, he still wasn't sure how he'd landed in bed with her after one of his monthly business trips to Adelaide to check on the store. All he could remember was being drawn relentlessly to Jessica in one the most intense connections of personal chemistry he'd ever experienced. Sexual attraction had blown away his intentions of keeping the stunning store manager at a healthy distance. After a year of illicit monthly bouts of passion, the role of manager of the Sydney store had become vacant and he'd persuaded Jessica, despite her reluctance, to take the transfer to the flagship store.

"What do you mean?"

"Oh, come on." Kim rolled her eyes. "This is me, Kimberley, your sister you're talking to. That distant facade doesn't cut it with me. And you're old enough to be starting to think about needing a wife…a family."

Ryan felt his lips twitch at his sister's irreverence. Then he said, "What makes you so certain that I'd want a wife like Jessica?"

"I know there's something between you two. Don't worry, I'm not going to pry. But she's bright and pretty—and she's doing a great job with the Sydney store. Look after her so that she doesn't decide to give up on you."

At his ferocious frown Kimberley pulled a face. "I just want you happy."

"I'm not into commitment, nor do I want a family."

"Oh." Kim's exclamation held a wealth of understanding. "Does Jessica know that?"

"Yes," he bit out.

"So there is something going on between you!"

His glare at Kimberley intensified. "You think you're so smart! Getting back together with Ric has given you the wedding bug. Why don't you find—" he looked around a trifle desperately "—Briana or Danielle or even Aunt Sonya a spouse?"

"Okay, I can take the hint. I'll mind my own business and leave you alone."

But after Kimberley had moved away with her nose stuck pointedly in the air Ryan found himself pondering what she'd said. *Look after her so that she doesn't decide to give up on you.*

Was Jessica dissatisfied? There'd been that argument they'd had about his spending Christmas at the Byron Bay beach house without her. She'd wanted to spend Christmas with him, but he'd been determined to spend the time with Howard to follow up on the discussions on how his own role within the company could be enlarged. Romance had been the last thing on his mind over the festive season. Jessica had sulked and spent time away with her parents instead. Then, in January, there'd been those horrific hours after his father's death when he'd been unable to locate her. And tangled in that had been the terrible suspicion that he'd never dared think about. Even now he thrust it from his mind.

If he thought back over the past month he'd have to say that she'd been quieter, more reflective, but he'd been so tied up in the catastrophe of his father's death—and the struggle to hold Blackstone's together in the face of all the public scandal—that he'd barely noticed. Perhaps he *was* too distant with Jessica.

But she'd always been so understanding.

And they were both so involved in their careers. That was one of the things that had drawn him to her. She didn't cling. Or demand. She was happy with what they had…or at least that was what he'd always believed.

Until Kim had started confusing him.

Did Jessica want more from him? And could he offer more? He shook his head. *No.* He'd never wanted a family.

But if Jessica was unhappy…

That was the last thing he'd wanted. He liked her…a lot. Perhaps he had been unfair to demand she keep their relationship a secret. Would she be happier if it were public knowledge? That certainly didn't mean he'd be marrying her. But if she were unhappy, that might go some of the way to stemming her dissatisfaction.

If Jessica didn't work for him it would be much easier. He'd been concerned about that from the outset, mostly because he hadn't wanted the kind of rumours that had surrounded his father. The endless, lewd speculation about his "secretaries." But Jessica was a hardly a secretary, she was a very capable store manager. If she didn't work for Blackstone's it would all be a lot simpler.

Across the room he could see a waiter offering her a glass of champagne, and Jessica's smiled refusal. He couldn't ask her to give up her career at Blackstone's, to go work somewhere else, simply because he didn't want to be seen sleeping with his store manager. Just the thought of letting her go disturbed him far more than he cared to admit.

Yet if his sister had worked out there was something between them, it wouldn't be long before others did, too. Jessica had moved in with him and had sublet her apartment—after much persuading from him. Sooner or later someone was going to discover that.

Ryan rubbed his jaw. There would be gossip. Endless media speculation. But did it really matter that much what people thought of him sleeping with his staff?

He started to cross the room to where Jessica still stood talking to Briana, the beautiful brunette whom half the men in the room would give their eye-teeth to meet. Yet it was Jessica's delicate features that held him captive. He'd almost reached them when an immaculately manicured hand settled on his arm.

"Ryan, so sorry about your father." Kitty Lang skipped to keep up with him, her long gold earrings swinging wildly beneath the bleached-blonde curls. "I heard that he left a fortune to that Marise Davenport." She tapped his arm and gave him an arch look. "Howard was always a bit of a ladies' man." Her giggle grated. "She worked for him a couple of years ago, didn't she?"

Ryan stopped and examined Kitty warily. "Marise worked for Blackstone's—in the marketing department. Not for Howard personally," he bit out, hating the way she made the word *work* sound. No doubt there was a good dose of the green-eyed monster at work. Kitty was rumoured to have been one of his father's mistresses. Not that Ryan paid much attention to the speculation. He'd learned long ago to try and ignore it.

"He always did have an eye for a pretty girl. And so much easier when they worked for Blackstone's. Keep it on the payroll."

His stomach turned. With distaste, he started to extricate himself from Kitty's clutches. This kind of talk was exactly why he hadn't gone public with his relationship with Jessica. The boss-sleeping-with-employee thing was so sordid. He'd been saying for years that Blackstone's should have a no-love-at-work contract.

Yet he'd have broken it.

"It wouldn't surprise me if Marise was already on her way out and that pretty little blonde was warming Howard's bed. He always liked blondes." Kitty ruffled a hand through her platinum curls. "And she works for Blackstone's, doesn't she?"

Something tightened in Ryan's gut. He went on red alert, every nerve end quivering. "Who are you talking about?"

"That girl."

"Which one?"

He followed where Kitty was pointing.

Jessica. "Jessica has never worked for my father." She worked for him! Let Kitty dare try intimate Jessica was one of his father's "secretaries."

"I saw them." Kitty wore an expression of catlike satisfaction.

"Where?" he challenged, praying that she'd spout some nonsense.

"I was flying a client on a charter to Fiji to look at a property." Kitty was a top-class realtor. "It was at the airport. They were arguing."

"That's it?" He stared at her. "That was enough for you to decide they were having an affair?"

"You had to see them together. It was their body language. The way she was talking to him. Lots of emotion. She was angry. But it was the kind of anger you only show someone you know very well."

Like a lover.

That's what Kitty meant.

But Jessica hardly knew his father. Ryan cast his mind back to the occasions he'd seen Jessica and his father in the same room during the eight years she'd worked for Blackstone's. Jessica went very quiet when his father was around. They never talked. No doubt Jessica had been a little in awe of his overpowering father.

Although he had to admit that after he'd discovered that Jessica was booked on the flight that went down he'd wondered why she'd been on the passenger list. Briefly. And he hated himself for the flare of suspicion. He'd suppressed it brutally for a whole month, refusing to even descend into the realm of those dark thoughts. Now Kitty was bringing it all back. He wasn't going there. Ryan sucked in a deep breath. "That means noth—"

"It was on the evening that Howard disappeared. He took her by the elbow, she struggled, then she went with him to board the jet."

"But she wasn't on the jet when it crashed." He tried to argue against what Kitty was saying. But it was getting harder. Jessica had been on the original passenger list. He'd nearly died when he'd seen that. And when he hadn't been able to reach her on her cell phone he'd assumed the worst....

And then he'd come home after the worst day of his life to find her watching television.

Giving himself a shake, Ryan turned away from Kitty, from the poison she was mouthing. Kitty must've made a mistake. Her convincing tale rang through his head. Perhaps she was lying...but why? She didn't know about him and Jessica.

He would ask Jessica about Kitty's allegations, and there would be a reasonable explanation. There had to be. He couldn't bear the alternative.

Jessica was pouring herself a cup of tea when he came up beside her.

"Would you like a cup?" she asked him.

Ryan noticed that she didn't look at him. No secret little smile. Nothing. She kept her attention firmly on the cup she was filling. How had this gap between him and Jessica developed? In future he was going to work on making her feel more valued. "I'll help myself to some coffee from the pot." He moved to the next table where one of the catering staff was filling cups with steaming coffee from a pot.

"Don't say that!" The irritated note in Jessica's voice behind him caught his attention. Jessica raising her voice? Ryan did a double take and turned his head. Jessica was standing with her hands on her hips, looking unmistakably annoyed.

"That's nothing more than vicious gossip. You should be careful what you say."

The target of her outburst had turned scarlet with mortification. What was Jessica so upset about? Ryan scanned the gathering. Briana had disappeared. Kitty was watching Jessica from a distance away, her mouth open in surprise. She caught Ryan's eye and mouthed *See?*

The tightness in his gut was back. Ryan rubbed his eyes. Had Kitty stumbled on the truth? Was his lover also his dead father's mistress?

Seated in the plush leather passenger seat of the BMW, Jessica tilted her head against the headrest and glanced across at Ryan. His hands were clenched on the steering wheel, leashing the torque of the powerful car, his knuckles white as he concentrated on the road ahead and his profile etched against the afternoon light, his nose long and straight, his hair springing back from the distinctive widow's peak.

The funeral was done.

She sighed.

"Tired?" he asked.

"A little." More than a little. Weariness seeped through her. Her feet were sore from standing around in high heels and her back ached. The nausea had returned, a reminder that it was time to start eating better for herself and the baby. She'd use her tiredness as an excuse tonight to sleep in the guest bedroom—as Ryan sometimes did when he came home late, so as not to wake her.

She had to find the strength to end it. She couldn't bear him to touch her tonight. Last night she'd said her goodbyes with every soft kiss, with every gentle stroke of her fingers. They would never make love again.

Never.

"What were you arguing with my father about on the day he died?"

His words slammed into her tired brain with all the force of a sledgehammer.

"Pardon?" Jessica hedged, and her heart lurched in her chest before starting to pound unsteadily. She'd hoped that Ryan would never learn about that awful confrontation.

"You were arguing with my father at the airport. I want to know what it was about."

You.

But she wouldn't tell Ryan that. He probably wouldn't believe her anyway. As much as she detested the man, Ryan idolized Howard Blackstone and strove to follow in his father's footsteps, even though she suspected that hidden behind Ryan's ruthless veneer had been a need for his father's respect.

"It wasn't exactly an argument." She crossed her fingers. "We were just talking."

"The person who saw you said it looked very personal— very emotive. Like you knew each other very well."

Oh, God.

This discussion she didn't need. Not now, not after the funeral. Ryan deserved good memories of his father—not her tainted, far-from-impartial opinion of Howard Blackstone.

She stalled. "Who told you we were arguing?"

"It doesn't matter." He shot her a frowning glance before directing his attention back to the road.

It doesn't matter. Jessica looked away, staring out the side window. For the past two years she'd lived in a fool's paradise. While she'd never expected a proposal of marriage when she'd moved into Ryan's penthouse a year ago, she'd certainly fantasized that Ryan would come to love her. The attraction between them had been so strong, so fierce and overwhelming from the first, that she'd been so sure love would follow.

Heck, she loved him. That's why she'd given in to Ryan's

urging and applied for the store manager's position of the Sydney store when it had come available. Even though she'd worried a little that she'd only gotten the job because she was sleeping with the boss. And even though Sydney was the last city in the world where she wanted to live.

She'd made the move so that she could spend more time with him. But she'd never expected his insistence that their affair remain a secret. And after a year she was still no more than a millionaire's hole-in-the-corner mistress.

Since her return, he never invited anyone over—not even his sister, certainly not his father. When she'd asked why no one visited, he'd told her that he valued his privacy and that he saw enough of his family at work. He had his own social life, his own set of friends he met for dinner in exclusive restaurants, a life he lived without her.

No more! She touched her belly. It wasn't about *her* anymore. Now she had a baby to think about. A child who deserved more than life on the outer edges of Ryan Blackstone's existence.

"You were having an affair with him." Ryan interrupted her thoughts.

Frowning, she tried to make sense of what he was saying. "Who's having an affair?"

"You!" he said, his voice harsh with impatience and anger. "*You* were having an affair with my father."

Three

'What?"

Jessica stared at Ryan in shock. The ugly accusation hung between them. Jessica had a feeling of being a distance away and seeing Ryan as if for the first time. Of looking at a total stranger.

"You honestly believe I was sleeping with your father?" She almost laughed in disbelief. It was so utterly off base. "You're joking, right?"

"No, I'm deadly serious." He slowed to a stop at the traffic light and pulled up the handbrake with unnecessary force. He flashed her a dark, smouldering glare, full of hard suspicion and anger. The tight set of his mouth and the tic in his jaw revealed his perturbation.

Jessica's heart sank. He did believe it. This wasn't some sick joke.

How the heck was she supposed to react to this bombshell?

She wanted to rage at him, scream, get out the car and storm off into the baking afternoon heat. But she suppressed the melodramatics that weren't her style. Struggling with her own anger, she aimed for a composure she was far from feeling. "You have some basis for this?"

"That's all you can say? Ask me if I have evidence?"

Jessica remained mute, refusing to be drawn further, refusing to defend herself against such a ghastly accusation. The silence turned icy.

The light changed to green and the car moved slowly forward. With a curse, Ryan pulled off the road and raked his fingers through his hair. Then he turned sideways in his seat to face her. "I'm trying to give you the benefit of the doubt."

"That's big of you." Jessica couldn't stop the sarcasm slipping out. It was clear that beneath the benefit of the doubt he'd given her, suspicion still lurked. Insulting, unspeakable suspicions that make her feel soiled and sick to the stomach.

"I even dismissed Kitty's comments as troublemaking—"

"Kitty!" Jessica felt no surprise. Kitty Lang was every bit as catty as her name suggested.

"So was it a lover's quarrel that Kitty witnessed? Was my father breaking it off with you, to take up with Marise? Or was he having an affair with Marise all along and you found out about it and confronted him?"

"I'm not answering that." Jessica had no intention of telling him what the fight with Howard had been about.

"Have you got nothing more to say?"

She shrugged. "You've made up your mind that Kitty's told you the truth, so what do you want me to say?"

"Tell me it's not true." But his eyes were watchful, weighing her every movement, and Jessica knew that he would pick apart any avowal of innocence. An ugly, cold, hollowness seeped through her.

She shook her head. "What's the point? You clearly don't trust me and haven't for some time, if you've had suspicions about this." Pain sliced into her soul. That he even had to ask her whether it was true shattered her, enraged her. She wouldn't stoop to offering an explanation.

"At least tell me that it wasn't you talking to my father at the airport that night."

Blood started to pound through her head at his insistence. She couldn't give him the reassurance he sought.

After a moment he sighed. "You were supposed to fly to Auckland the afternoon before the crash on a commercial carrier, for the opening of the new store the next day. You didn't go. All you ever told me was that you'd changed your mind. I shoved aside the fact that that your name was on the passenger list for my father's flight. I dismissed it as a clerical error, a glitch in the bookings with several employees going to Auckland. With my father dead, I was too damned relieved that you hadn't flown that night. But I think you did change your flight. You decided to fly with my father…and then for some reason you never went."

She stared at him, her heart thudding in her chest, and said nothing. She'd missed the commercial flight, and the rest of the flights had been booked solid. She'd waitlisted herself for several of them, waiting at the airport on standby, watching each darn plane take off into the night sky. Spending several hours in Howard Blackstone's revolting company on the flight to Auckland had been a last resort…until she'd seen Howard while they were boarding, heard what he'd had to say. No way in hell had she been prepared to spend time in Howard's company after that altercation.

But Ryan didn't deserve an explanation. Her hands knotted in her lap; her nails dug into her palms. Ryan could believe what he damn well wanted. She no longer cared.

"That's it? That's what caused your suspicions? A change of flight?" She tried to laugh it away.

He hesitated, then his gaze hardened. "More the fact that you never bothered to let me know about your change in plans."

Jessica turned her head and stared blindly out the side window. She and Ryan had argued. She'd wanted to spend Christmas with him, but it hadn't suited him. They hadn't spoken while they'd been apart—she'd been upset. Then, while staying with her parents, she'd found out she was pregnant. And suddenly she had to decide how she was going to deal with it all.

No cats. No kids. No press. No diamond ring.

Those were his terms for their affair. By the end of the holiday she'd known she had only one choice: to break it off with him. She'd intended to take a couple of days off after the opening of the Auckland store to give her time to shore up the courage, and end their affair on her return to Sydney.

Except she'd never made it to Auckland.

And then his father's plane had gone missing.

Afterwards everything had come apart. It had taken ages for the search-and-rescue team to find his father's body. Ryan had been so distraught that Jessica couldn't bring herself to desert him in case he needed her. And knowing how he felt about commitment, there was no way in the world that she could tell him about the baby.

But now the end had come. Because Ryan Blackstone needed no one—least of all her.

"Hey," Ryan caught Jessica's arm as they exited the elevator into his two-storied penthouse apartment and pulled her around to face him. "Don't retreat into silence. We need to talk this out."

Deep down he clung to the growing hope, fuelled by her

angry reaction, that she hadn't betrayed him, hadn't been his
father's mistress.

Jessica was his.

Surely she knew that.

His body certainly recognised her as his woman. His
fingers had unconsciously started to move, to knead the soft,
silken skin below her elbow. Standing this close, he was surrounded by the scent of roses from her perfume, heady and
intensely feminine. Already his body was hardening, in tune
with every breath she took, aware of every move she made.
As soon as she'd explained everything to his satisfaction,
they would kiss and make up.

He could barely wait.

His blood was already pumping a little faster through his
veins as the primal lust she aroused so effortlessly took hold.
He wondered if they'd have time to make it to the bedroom
or whether he'd take her here on the carpeted stairs.

But first she owed him an explanation.

A little shard of unease pierced him.

What if Jessica *had* been his father's lover? Would he be
able to forgive her? He comforted himself that the fantastic
sex they shared would have to be enough. He'd just watch her
very carefully in the future, keep her satiated so that she had
no need to stray ever again. He told himself that the bitter
emotion the thought of Jessica with his father aroused was
nothing more than rage at her betrayal. He could get over that.
He would forgive her. As long as she understood it must never
happen again.

"I want the truth, Jessica. Then afterwards…" His voice
trailed away, but he could feel the betraying heat glaze his
eyes, the voracious hunger tighten his muscles until he felt
he might snap.

"Afterwards?" Her face was cold. Frozen. "What do you

mean *afterwards*? After accusing me of having an affair with your father, you think I want to screw—"

"Hey, calm down." He leashed the annoyance that flashed through him. Surely Jessica knew that what they shared was more than that. But he'd never seen her like this. So passionless. Hard. He loosened his grip on her arm and stroked his fingers over her skin. He glimpsed the sheen of tears. Then she blinked and the veil of moisture was gone.

Jessica slapped his arm away. "Don't touch me!" Her voice cracked and she swung around and headed for the stairs.

"Where are you going?"

"To pack."

"Pack?" Disbelief rolled through him. "What do you mean pack?"

She turned, a hand on the banister, and looked down at him. "It's over, Ryan. It's been over for a long time. But I was too stupid to notice."

Two steps took him to the bottom step. "What do you mean it's over? You can't leave—"

"Watch me. I'm going to walk out the penthouse, out your life and—"

"Out my life?" Alarm bells rang loudly in his head. What the hell had gotten into Jessica? "What about Blackstone's? What about your job?" And what about making love with him?

She stopped at the top of the stairs. "It's always about Blackstone's, isn't it? You don't have a heart, Ryan, you have a glittering lump of carbon inside you. Don't worry, I'll stay. I'll help Kimberley arrange the launch of the Something Old, Something New collection at the end of the month. I won't leave you in the lurch. But in a couple of months I'll be moving on. So start looking for someone to replace me."

Replace her? He stared up at her, aghast. How could he ever replace her?

"Wait." She couldn't simply walk out. He needed her. "You can't do this."

"Watch me." She raised her chin.

Jessica had a soft heart. She was a pushover. "My father was buried today. Doesn't that mean anything to you?"

"Because I'm supposed to be his mistress?"

"No—" He searched for the right words. Had his father dumped her? If so, his instincts to keep his relationship with her secret had been good. What a ghastly scandal there would've been if it had come out that both he and his father had been sleeping with the same woman. A woman who worked for Blackstone's. God! What a mess.

"I'm very sorry for your loss, Ryan." Her face was set and pale. "Hard as you may find it to believe, I never saw much to admire in your father. He was arrogant and conceited, and he had an appalling view of women."

"You sound as if you hated him," Ryan said slowly, trying to read her expression beneath the stony anger.

Jessica blinked. "Not hate."

"Then what?"

Jessica hesitated. "Despise. I despised him. I became your mistress despite your father. Why do you think I never argued when you never offered to take me to your family gatherings?" She gave him a twisted smile.

Ryan eyed that smile. There was a lot more to her relationship with his father than met the eye. Maybe his suspicions had been misguided…but then why hadn't Jessica set him straight?

"I didn't want to spend my precious free time with a bastard like Howard Blackstone," she continued, her usually tender eyes flashing. "Do you know what's really funny?"

"What?" Ryan asked warily, certain he wasn't going to find the answer at all amusing.

"I became your lover despite your father's terrible reputation for bedding his secretaries. I told myself you were different, that you were nothing like your father—"

"He struggled to come to terms with my mother's death, he loved her. My father was a great man."

"Was he?" She lifted an eyebrow.

"Howard Blackstone built a successful empire. He was a well-known humanitarian."

"He was a terrible father. He made more enemies than friends." Jessica ticked Howard's shortcomings off on her fingers. "Believe me there is no woman less likely than I to be your mistress. For more than a year I've lived with you here, been your kept woman, but it's over. I'll never be any man's mistress again."

Ryan stared at her. Had Jessica expected him to *marry* her? Hell! He'd liked her, enjoyed her company and absolutely lived to make love to her, but he had no intention of marrying anyone. She knew that. She'd accepted that. "If this is about getting a marriage proposal out of me, then it *is* over." Ryan flung the words at her. "Because I don't want—or need—a wife. I told you that at the outset."

Jessica gave a snort from the top of the stairs. She disappeared into the room they'd shared and Ryan decided to wait downstairs. He picked up a newspaper and settled down in his favourite chair. She'd calm down, he told himself as he heard the muffled sounds of movement upstairs. It would all blow over.

Ten minutes later she reappeared, carrying a suitcase. "I'll send someone over for the rest of my things," she said over her shoulder as she strode past.

Dropping the paper, he rose to his feet. "Jessica, you need to think this through."

She hit the button for the elevator. "I've thought of nothing else for months."

Months? He did a double take. "If you walk into that elevator it's over. I won't come running after you."

"I don't expect you to." The doors slid silently open. Without a backward glance, she walked into the waiting cage.

The organ that Jessica had referred to as a glittering lump of carbon felt a pang of something…something Ryan could identify only as regret.

The board meeting Ryan had been waiting for with such eager anticipation was over.

Without looking at the other board members, Ryan made his escape, desperate for space and a reprieve from the arctic air-conditioning. Shoving his hands in his pockets he walked out of the impressive building that housed Blackstone Diamonds' head office and jostled with lunchtime shoppers on Pitt Street who had taken advantage of the Monday lull to visit a host of boutiques in the nearby malls.

When he'd come back from golf on Saturday and sailing on Sunday, Jessica had not been waiting at the penthouse with her ready smile and soft voice. A sense of emptiness had nagged at him all weekend. The penthouse had seemed sterile and the music he'd played on his state-of-the-art sound system had echoed hollowly around the immaculate interior. There'd been no relaxing out on the balcony overlooking the harbour as the sun sank, while the wind tugged at Jessica's tousled hair.

But Ryan refused to be emotionally blackmailed. She would come around.

As for this morning's meeting, it had been disastrous. Ryan's blood still boiled at the memory. He'd argued that public confidence demanded that a Blackstone be chairman of the board—particularly with the company under threat of a takeover from Matt Hammond, Kimberley's former boss.

His uncle Vincent had agreed.

But the rest of the board had not felt the same way. Ric Perrini had gotten the chairmanship he had coveted.

"Ric may not be a Blackstone, but his loyalty is not in question. He has far and away the most experience, and he's married to a Blackstone." The words of one of the directors still rang in Ryan's ears.

And his sister had hovered, halfway down the table, clearly torn between wanting to stand by her husband and to maintain the truce with him.

The old seething resentment against his brother-in-law was back in full force. But at the forefront of Ryan's mind as he stalked down the street was the determination that tonight he would not return to an empty penthouse.

He rounded the corner into Martin Place, and continued until he reached the discreetly elegant Blackstone's signage outside the imposing facade of the heritage building that housed the largest and most profitable of all the jewellery stores he controlled.

At least the stores were a success no one could take from him. His vision and planning had led to increased profits, expansion and new stores and designs for jewellery that the market loved.

With a nod he strode past Nathaniel, the liveried doorman who had worked here for the past ten years, through the revolving doors and into the airy gallery-style ground floor, empty of everything except a towering modern black marble sculpture in the centre and glass display cabinets built into the walls.

An incisive glance revealed that a batch of pale pink diamonds recently cut in New York had already been set in modern settings of white gold and placed in the wall-mounted display boxes. Ryan paused. The pieces looked stunning. Yes, they would whet the appetite of the discerning shopper.

The best and biggest stones mined at the Blackstone-owned Janderra mine were still sent to Antwerp for cutting and were available for inspection only by appointment.

The surge of pride for all he'd achieved took him by surprise. He was responsible for the glittering success of the stores. Even his father had known that....

After the humiliating defeat he'd just suffered in the boardroom, he would make the launch of the stunning collections timed for the Northern Hemisphere summer so magnificent that the cognoscenti would be talking about it for months.

Buoyed with new-found enthusiasm, he made for the impressive stairway that led to the next floor—where the majority of walk-in business was conducted.

At the top of the stairwell lay the salon-style showroom, with its thick marbled columns and glittering crystal chandeliers, redolent with the rich patina of wealth.

Ryan's gaze landed on Jessica and he froze. She was facing away from him, talking to Holly McLeod, a PR assistant involved in helping with the organisation of the Something Old, Something New showing that would take place in the spacious downstairs lobby later in the month.

Jessica hadn't contacted him over the weekend to collect her possessions. By now, with time to cool down, she'd surely have realized the tactical mistake she'd made. By tonight he was determined to have her back in his bed—where she belonged.

At the thought, his hormones went wild, and he gave her a very subtle, intensely sexual once-over. She was wearing a silky blouse in an oyster shade and a pair of smartly tailored pale grey linen trousers cool enough for the Sydney heat. A strand of lustrous pearls at her neck and a pair of snakeskin heels high enough to be sexy completed the outfit that managed to strike a balance between stylish and sensual.

She reminded him of the pale pink diamonds he'd been

admiring downstairs, so cool and impervious on the outside but inside the fire sparkled with a brilliance that was breathtaking.

Ryan reined back the raw need that the sight of her unleashed. He would handle her with care, with a fine meal and plenty of flattery. He couldn't afford for her to walk out of her job—not with the show so close. Jessica was too sensible to walk away from Blackstone's. She'd never allow her personal life to jeopardise her future. Her career would always come first.

They were similar in that outlook.

But he didn't need to stand here and stare at her all day. Jessica was his lover. He knew every inch of her covered flesh intimately.

Ryan strolled forward. "Jessica, a moment, please."

She turned her head. Ryan found himself staring into blank, polite brown eyes. "Good morning, Ryan."

The chilly formality took him aback. "I need to talk to you." He glanced at Holly. "Privately."

But Holly was already moving away, the picture of efficiency in a tailored white shirt and black trousers, her long dark hair caught up in a sleek ponytail, a leather folder clasped to her chest.

"Look, about Friday night—"

"If this is not work-related then I'd rather not discuss it right now. I have details I need to finalise with Holly."

She started after Holly. Ryan reached out and grabbed her. It didn't take a rocket scientist to know that Jessica was signalling that this conversation was at an end.

"I have work to do!"

As she spun to face him, Ryan stared at her, flummoxed. Jessica had never spoken to him in that sharp voice. Even during working hours when they'd kept each other at a professional distance—at his insistence—she hadn't been this distant. He let her arm go.

Alarm fluttered through him. For the first time he considered the possibility that he might've lost her—that she really wouldn't be coming back.

He regrouped rapidly. "Let's have lunch—"

"I'm really busy, Ryan."

"Dinner then."

"I'm going to my parents for dinner tonight."

He'd imagined she'd be staying with her parents. If not, where the hell was she staying? He'd find out tonight. "What time will you be finished? I'll pick you up, and we can go for a drink first—" He broke off as she shook her head.

"I'm bringing Picasso back with me. I can't leave him alone on his first night at my apartment."

Picasso? His frown deepened. Who the hell was Picasso? Oh, yes, her rag-bag cat.

No pets. No kids. No press. No diamond rings. Those had been the ground rules of their affair. He wasn't sure which item on the list he detested most. They all reeked of the insidious ways that women curtailed a man's freedom. If he'd allowed the cat, the designer elegance of the penthouse would've been transformed into off-the-rack homeliness before he'd had time to take a breath. The excuse that he hadn't wanted the animal in his penthouse in case it wrecked the expensive furnishings had worked. Now she was taking it back to her apartment….

Her apartment?

He stiffened. "I thought you'd sublet your apartment?"

"No." She met his gaze levelly. "You ordered me to sublet it and assumed I had. I wanted to keep it available. I wasn't sure when I'd need it."

Her words rocked him. She'd been expecting this. Months,

she'd said on Friday night. *I've thought of nothing else for months.*

Why? Why had she planned to break it off? If it hadn't been because of his father, then who? He cast his mind back, trying to remember any man she'd mentioned, talked about. No one attracted a red flag. But then she had her own social life, as he had his. "Is there someone else?"

"Of course not!" Her eyes were flashing.

He pushed away the festering thought of Jessica with his father. "You're telling me no other party is involved in our breakup?"

Her gaze slid away from his. "Why the postmortem, Ryan?" Then her breath caught and the eyes that snapped back to his were filled with remorse. "Sorry, that was tactless."

She was hiding something. There was someone. He reached for her hand. "Jessica—"

"Not at work, Ryan." She yanked her fingers free. "Someone might see."

The tingle from the brush of her fingers against his lingered. He shoved his hand into his pocket and stared at her through narrowed eyes. After a moment he dismissed the half-formed suspicion that she was mocking him and swivelled to scan the room. "No one is looking."

It occurred to him that he had no clue what was going on inside her beautiful blonde head. Suddenly he wished he hadn't insisted on their maintaining separate sets of friends, separate social lives. But then he'd never expected *her* to be the one to break it off.

God, how had this happened? Of all the countless beautiful women he'd dated, how had this one managed to get under his guard?

"Meet me for dinner tomorrow then, after work."

"To discuss work?"

"No, to talk about us."

"There is no 'us.' It's over, Ryan." She gave an impatient sigh and brushed the blonde tendrils off her face. Then she hurried away, calling Holly's name, and he stared after her.

An icy determination filled his gut. Ryan tilted his head to one side and narrowed his gaze as he considered his options. He couldn't do anything about losing the chairmanship of the board…yet. But he was damned if he would lose Jessica.

That afternoon Jessica couldn't get Ryan's bleak expression out of her mind as she flipped through a brochure featuring carefully selected pieces of the Something Old, Something New collections being launched at the end of the month.

It certainly wasn't because she'd left him.

More likely it was the realisation that his father was gone forever that had turned his handsome features into a haggard mask. She couldn't help feeling guilty about breaking it off with him.

But she'd had no choice.

It was best for herself…and her baby. After all, what did she want with a man who made it clear that he wanted nothing more than a secret mistress—one whom he believed could leap into bed with his father?

But it was the best solution for Ryan, too. With all the problems facing Blackstone's, the last thing Ryan needed right now was the additional scandal of a pregnant secret mistress erupting in the public eye.

Nor was she ready to tell him about the baby yet. She couldn't bear for him to accuse her of deliberately getting pregnant. Or ask her to abort the child he would never want. It was her problem, not his. And she wanted this baby, *his* baby, with a desperation that astonished her.

She turned the page, and stopped at the glossy photo of a stunning Xander Safin piece. Quickly she made a call to Xander and arranged a time to meet him in two days to show him how magnificently the brochures had come out.

When Holly returned later with the next pile of brochures to show her Jessica was unprepared for Holly's question. "Did you read the memo from head office?"

She searched Holly's blue-green eyes for a clue. "What memo?"

"The e-mail memo announcing that the chairmanship has been decided."

Tiredly Jessica brushed her hair off her face and dropped her gaze to stare blindly at the brochure. *The chairmanship of the board*. The position that Ryan had wanted most in the world.

"I've been so busy I haven't had a chance to go through my e-mails yet. What was the outcome?" She waited, tensing. He'd lost so much with his father's death, she couldn't bear it if he lost this, too.

"Ric Perrini was voted in."

Jessica squeezed her eyes shut. Then a horrible thought struck her. Her eyes snapped open. "When?" Then more urgently she asked, "When did this happen?"

"This morning. Just before lunch."

Jessica swore softly.

Holly looked at her with a slightly startled expression.

Ryan must have come straight from the board meeting to the store. He'd asked her to lunch. And she'd sent him away. Had he come to share what must've been a devastating blow with her? Then the next realisation hit her. *That* must be the reason he'd looked so terrible. Nothing to do with their breakup. Nothing to do with her at all. It was all about Blackstone's.

Holly was playing with a small solitaire pendant that hung

from a gold chain around her neck. "He'll be okay. Ryan is such an iceman, nothing gets to him."

Jessica blinked. Was that how people saw Ryan? As an iceman? Was she the only one who saw beneath the diamond-hard exterior to the volcanic emotions below? The anger. The passion. The mix of turbulent emotions that made up the complex man she loved but did not always understand.

Holly looked concerned. "I really thought you knew."

"Don't worry about it. I'll read the e-mail later. I'm glad you told me. I'm sure Ryan will be disappointed. But Ric will make a fine chairman."

By the following day, everyone knew that Ric Perrini was now chairman of the board, and Jessica's heart ached for Ryan. But she wouldn't allow herself to weaken and call him to offer sympathy. She had to think of herself first now, and their baby.

She didn't see him that day—too much must be happening up at the corporate office in Pitt Street. But when she got home after swimming at the local pool in the hope that exercise might help her sleep better tonight in her lonely double bed, it was to Picasso's frantic complaints—and her newly activated answerphone blinking.

Ryan.

Jessica's first thought was of him.

Then she remembered that Ryan didn't even have this number. The message was from her mother, to whom she'd given her number earlier in the day. When Jessica pulled her cell phone out of her Fendi bag, she saw she'd missed four calls from him during the afternoon. She sank into a chair and put her head in her hands. Who was she kidding? Finally, she picked up the handset and punched in the cell phone number she knew by heart.

"I heard about the chairmanship, I'm sorry. Is that why you came down to the store? To tell me?"

"That's why you called me?" he asked. "To commiserate?"

After that crack, she wasn't telling him that she'd been worried sick about him. "Why else?"

"I see." He sounded strange.

"Ryan...?" He didn't respond. "Do you want me to come over?"

"Come over or come back?"

"I'm not coming back." A deafening silence met her stark statement. Jessica bit her lip. Should she have softened her refusal? No. There was no going back. Not to what they'd had. And Ryan wasn't capable of offering her more.

Then he sighed softly. "Don't worry about coming over. I don't need pity right now."

Pity? Jessica nearly told him exactly what had almost been on offer. Her body...her heart...her soul. Their baby.

Fool. Ryan Blackstone certainly didn't need a ready-made family—or her love!

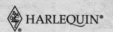

COMING NEXT MONTH

#1855 MISTRESS & A MILLION DOLLARS—
Maxine Sullivan
Diamonds Down Under
He will stop at nothing to get what he wants. And if it costs him a million dollars to make her his mistress...so be it!

#1856 IRON COWBOY—Diana Palmer
Long, Tall Texans
He was as ornery as they come. But this billionaire Texan didn't stand a chance of escaping the one woman who was his match... in every way.

#1857 BARGAINING FOR KING'S BABY—Maureen Child
Kings of California
He agreed to marry his rival's daughter to settle a business deal... but she has her own bargain for her soon-to-be husband. Give her a baby or lose the contract!

#1858 THE SPANISH ARISTOCRAT'S WOMAN—
Katherine Garbera
Sons of Privilege
She was only supposed to play the count's lover for one day. But suddenly, she's become his wife.

#1859 CEO'S MARRIAGE SEDUCTION—Anna DePalo
It was the perfect plan. Wed her father's business protégé and have the baby she's been dreaming about...until scandals threaten her plan for the perfect marriage of convenience.

#1860 FOR BLACKMAIL...OR PLEASURE—Robyn Grady
Blackmailing his ex-fiancée into working for him was easy. Denying the attraction still between them could prove to be lethal.

SDCNM0208

Four

The following evening Ryan came to an abrupt stop on the threshold of the Louvre Bar, where he'd invited Ric and his sister for a truce-sealing after-work drink to celebrate Ric's appointment as chairman of the board. After a day spent soul-searching, he decided it was time to put his disappointment behind him, and throw his support behind Ric.

He'd arrived early. And the sight of two pale heads close together caused his teeth to clench until his jaw hurt.

Jessica and Xander Safin?

Was Xander the reason why Jessica had ditched him? For the first time Ryan considered Xander as a man rather than Blackstone's hotshot jewellery designer. Tall and lean. Indisputably good-looking with high Slavic cheekbones that gave his features an exotic mysticism that few women would be able to resist.

Too engrossed in each other, neither of them had seen Ryan. Right now Xander sat far too close to Jessica for Ryan's liking, his pale grey eyes sparkling and his hands moving expressively in the air as he spoke, while Jessica listened, nodding and interjecting the occasional comment.

Jessica's ability to listen was the quality that singled her out from every woman Ryan had ever known. And he missed the companionable silences. Jessica made it easy to relax, to be himself.

Hell, it had been less than a week and already he missed all that.

Ryan found an empty booth and dropped down onto the leather bench seat. From this angle he could still see them. He hadn't even known she saw Xander outside work. But when Jessica said something that caused Xander to fling his head back and laugh out loud, it became evident that they were very much at ease in each other's company.

His own fault!

He'd been the one to insist that they maintain separate social lives. Even though he'd been totally faithful to Jessica during their time together, he hadn't wanted a clinging vine when he finally ended their relationship. And now his separate-space philosophy had come back to bite him in the ass.

Jessica was an attractive, intelligent woman. No doubt there was a queue of men waiting to take his place. Starting with Xander-bloody-Safin.

Ryan found he didn't care for that idea at all.

"What's Jessica doing with him?"

He glanced up to find Ric sliding into the booth opposite him holding two beers, one of which he slid across the table. Ryan took it with a nod of thanks and looked around for his sister.

Before he could reprimand Kim, she'd rushed into speech. "I didn't tell him. Promise. He worked it out."

Ryan swallowed his annoyance. "I suppose it makes my reaction to you two—" his glance took in Kim and Ric "—all those years ago seem completely hypocritical?"

"Is that why you took such pains to hide your affair with Jessica?" Ric's gaze was fearsomely direct. "You didn't want it known that you were sleeping with the staff, when you've always been so vocally against it?"

"Relationships in companies always cause tension." Damn, but he sounded pious.

"Not always." Kim smiled slowly at Ric.

Ryan envied the easy confidence between them, the love that his sister deserved. "Just look at Dad."

"He'd fire his secretaries when they took his attentions too seriously." Kim shook her head. "Those poor women."

"Exactly. And his office would be in chaos for weeks."

"So why did you start something with Jessica if you knew that you'd probably end up firing her...if she's fool enough to fall in love with you?"

His sister's words hit him in the gut. Jessica, in love with him? No chance of that. Especially not after he'd accused her of sleeping with his father. And if his accusation had been wrong, then she'd have every right to be hurt and disappointed in his lack of trust. If he'd screwed that up, would she ever let him close again?

For a moment Ryan contemplated ignoring his sister's question. Then he shrugged. "I thought this time would be different. That I could control it." Hell, he'd gotten that wrong.

"Like you control everything else?"

Ryan glared at her, and she held her hands up. "Okay, I take that back."

"It was never intended to be anything more than a temporary affair. Jessica knew that. I knew Dad wouldn't approve of the relationship, either. He's always made it clear that I needed to think with my head when it came to women. Connections are—were—important to Dad."

"Because her family's not wealthy?" Kim asked. "That's

ridiculous. She runs the Sydney store with formidable acumen, she has an eye for design, she knows what the consumer wants and she has flair. Fashion nous."

"I never realised you were such a fan."

His sister drew an audible breath, then said quietly, "We've spent a lot of time together in the last month. I'd like to think that I can count her as a friend."

"I'm sure Dad wouldn't have minded Jessica being my 'friend'—he had enough of those himself." Ryan's mouth curled. "But I don't think he would've been too happy to find out she was living in my penthouse."

"She's living with you?" Kim's eyes were wide. "Why the secrecy?"

"Then what's she doing here with Xander Safin?" Ric interjected.

Trust Ric to cut to the heart of it. "We broke up," Ryan confessed reluctantly.

"Oh, Ryan." Kimberley shook her head in aggravation and her dark hair swirled across her shoulders. "Sometimes you puzzle me. She's the best thing that could've happened to you…and you worry about what Dad would think?"

Maybe his sister was right. He'd behaved like a jerk. But he couldn't help saying defensively, "You know what it was like, Kim. Always having to do the right thing. You know the price of disappointing Howard Blackstone." For far too long he'd tried to be the son his father wanted. To win his father's approval. The time had come to live his life on his terms—and to stop being a Howard Blackstone clone.

Kim met his gaze. "Dad is dead. And we're not children anymore. I've told you before, you could do a lot worse than Jessica Cotter, little brother."

"That's probably academic. Because it doesn't look like

Ryan will get the chance." Ric tilted his head in the direction of the other couple.

Ryan's gaze cut across the bar in time to see Jessica reach up and place a kiss on Xander Safin's mouth.

Jealousy slashed through him. Damn them! Jessica had no right to be kissing other men. She belonged in his bed, not in Xander Safin's arms. Jessica was his woman—and his alone.

The anger at her desertion came back in full force. He tore his gaze away from the couple and looked into his brother-in-law's all-seeing eyes.

"Let's get the hell out of here, before I take him apart with my bare hands," he muttered, his throat raw. He'd known that *something* had happened to force her to end their relationship. Xander-bloody-Safin had happened.

He shook his head to clear it of the rage. How could she have turned to another man to match the passion that they'd shared? Or had she'd felt neglected. Had she believed that he was ashamed of her?

"No, need," Ric replied. "They're leaving. If you want her back you're going to have to move swiftly. She's clearly not going to sit around moping over you."

Dammit, Ric was right. He'd been hoping that she'd realise her mistake, that she'd cool down and come back. But seeing her so cosy with Xander caused Ryan to reassess. If he didn't move fast, he might lose her for good.

Jessica belonged to him. What he needed was a way to force her to spend time with him. And this time he'd do things differently. This time he'd make sure she was so enthralled that she wouldn't look at another man.

But right now Ryan could do little except watch as the woman he wanted more than all the pink diamonds in Janderra walked out the bar beside the tall blond jewellery designer, turning heads as they went.

* * *

Jessica found that the days had been spinning past, faster and faster. She was busy and the store buzzed with customers. On top of all that, helping with the organisation for the approaching jewellery show meant even more unrelenting pressure. Each night she returned to her apartment utterly exhausted. She put the extreme fatigue down to her pregnancy. But she knew it would all be worth it once the baby was born. She couldn't wait to hold the life that grew within her.

When she walked into the store on Friday morning, bracing herself for another long day before the weekend, the last thing she expected was to find Ryan waiting in her office, a cup of coffee cradled between his hands. He looked relaxed and perfectly at home in her domain. By contrast, she felt harassed, a little ill as the scent of the coffee reached her…and a lot late.

He unfolded his legs and rose to his feet as she entered.

"Don't worry about getting up." As always his perfect manners triggered a softness deep inside her.

Jessica subsided into her chair behind the desk. She'd just come from an appointment with her doctor. She'd mentioned her tiredness, the drained feeling and he'd upped her iron intake. When Dr. Waite told her that the nausea should start receding now that she was in the second trimester, she'd wanted to kiss the man in gratitude.

Then he'd told her that she could look forward to being a little absentminded in this trimester. Jessica had groaned aloud, thinking of all that needed to be done for the launch. She couldn't afford to be scatter-brained. Not now of all times.

As Ryan sat down again, Jessica turned on her computer and reached for her PalmPilot. "I don't remember that we had an appointment," she said pointedly.

"We don't." Ryan took a sip, his green eyes examining her over the top of his mug. "But I wanted to let you know before the others that I'll be moving down here for the next few weeks in preparation for the launch."

"Here? You'll be working here?" Jessica's heart sank.

He nodded. "Think about it. It makes perfect sense."

"But Kimberley's also involved and she's working out of head office." So why the heck was he moving down here? His constant presence was going to mess with her head.

"Kimberley is only involved with the publicity. Holly McLeod and a couple of others working with her are all based at Pitt Street, so it wouldn't be a good idea to move my sister down here." He rocked back in the chair and took another sip of coffee. "I want to be where the heartbeat is. The place where the show will take place. The place where our jewellery is displayed, where the customers visit."

"But where will you sit?" She tried to remain calm and rational and not reveal her utter horror at what he was saying to her. "You'll want somewhere quiet, where you can work. Most of the space here is taken up by the salon, a couple of appointment rooms, which are heavily used, the vaults and storage space. You certainly can't use the staff canteen." She didn't care if she sounded unwelcoming. She didn't want Ryan around all day long, a daily reminder of all that she had lost.

It would be too painful.

And it increased one hundredfold the chances of him discovering that she was pregnant.

He shrugged. "I'll find somewhere. There's a small boardroom next door that I can use."

"But the plugs are too far from the table to be any use for your laptop." She knew that Ryan never remembered to charge the batteries, and he hadn't gotten around to upgrading to wireless like the rest of the senior management team. "And there's no phone extension."

"I can use my cell phone." He peered sideways. "You have enough plugs here to run a power station. I can always share your office if I need to use my laptop."

Oh, no!

She'd moved out his penthouse, now he planned to move into her office. If it wasn't so upsetting, it might be farcical.

"I'll be out of town for some of the time. And you're on the floor a lot," he added. "There should be plenty of space for both of us."

She stared at him, aghast. She'd been spending her lunchtimes in her office with the door closed and her feet up to stop her ankles swelling in the heat. And she'd been taking short breaks through the day when the tiredness plagued her. With Ryan under her feet, it wouldn't take him long to start asking questions. Just the thought was enough to make her shudder with dread.

"Suit yourself. You're the boss." She looked away and tried to look unconcerned as she logged her password into the computer.

"I'm going to need your help, Jess."

Her heart ached at the tender, familiar way he spoke the shortened version of her name that only he used. "With what?"

"With the jewellery show." He hesitated, then said solemnly, "Some people are muttering that we should've cancelled the showing, given my father's tragic death. I think that those rumours were started by our competitors and the press have been eager to run with them. I want the show to be a tribute to my father, to be the best that's ever been done."

Put like that, how could she refuse? "Of course, I'll help you." Then she thought of something she'd been meaning to ring him about. "I'd like to collect my things over the weekend. Will tomorrow be convenient?" Since she still held a key to the penthouse, she could slip in sometime during the morning, while Ryan played his regular Saturday round of golf with a group of businessmen who held powerful jobs.

The silence stretched.

She glared at the computer screen. "Or perhaps next week some time?"

"Not next week, I'll be going to Janderra for part of the week so I won't be able to help you pack."

That caught her attention. "But what about the races?" The annual St. Valentine's Diamond Stakes, sponsored by Blackstone Diamonds, would be held next week in Melbourne. Jessica had been considering giving the event a wide berth this year. Prickles of tension spread across her skin. Last year she'd spent the day pretending to barely know Ryan and the night going wild in his arms....

"It would be a pity to miss that." She glanced at him, hoping that none of her memories showed in her eyes.

A frown pleated his brow. "I'm too busy to go to Melbourne. You can collect your possessions tomorrow, if you want."

He stood. Seconds later he was gone, taking his empty mug with him, and all of a sudden Jessica felt bereft. She placed her hand on her stomach. Earlier, she'd heard the baby's heartbeat. It had been noisy, although the doctor had said that part of the noise had been her own heartbeat in the background. But it had made everything so real, so thrilling.

And even though Ryan had always made it clear he had no intention of being a family man, what had been missing when she'd heard the baby's heartbeat had been Ryan at her side to share the wonder.

Jessica swiped the access card that controlled the elevator that went up to Ryan's Pyrmont penthouse apartment in the luxurious complex overlooking the harbour. It felt odd to be entering the elevator, riding up to the empty penthouse, the place where she'd lived in a temporary waiting-for-the-shoe-to-drop manner for the past year. Today would be the last time she'd come here.

The doors hissed open. She stepped out...and stopped dead.

Instead of the vacant apartment she'd expected, Ryan sat in the living room, the weekend papers scattered over the leather couch beside him. Dressed casually in a pair of black jeans and a white polo shirt, he looked unfairly breathtaking.

"You're supposed to be at golf," she accused, struggling to recover from the shock. *Why was he here?* His Saturday morning round of golf was sacred, he never missed it. Everywhere she turned lately, Ryan was there, larger than life, dominating *her* life.

"I thought you might come this morning." Was that a hint of satisfaction in those rich green eyes? "I skipped golf so that I could be here to help you."

"But—" Jessica broke off. She didn't need his help. She must look like a fish, with her mouth opening and closing as she tried to think of something to say. "You didn't need to do that," she said lamely.

"Oh, but I did." He swept the newspapers aside and rose to his feet. "You've lived here for a year. How could I let you leave like a thief in the night?" Despite the polite words, his eyes were full of turbulence.

Jessica gnawed at her lip. He was going to make this difficult. "I'll be fine, honestly." She glanced helplessly at her watch. "If you go now—"

"It's too late for me to play today."

"But you could still make the second nine—"

With the wave of his arm he dismissed the golf game, and

his mates. "I organised them a fourth already. They don't need me."

"Neither do I," she murmured rebelliously.

He stilled. "No, I don't suppose you do."

The edge of cynicism in his voice caused her to say, "What's that supposed to mean?"

"You have Xander Safin now to satisfy your…needs."

"That's a disgusting thing to say. Xander's a colleague. We have a working relationship."

"And you kiss all your colleagues?" His voice was soft, lethal.

Jessica blinked. Then she thought frantically what he could be talking about.

A kiss?

Of course! She'd kissed Xander goodbye the other night. "You should have come over and said hello rather than watching from wherever you were hiding. That was a good-night kiss to the friend that Xander has become."

He tipped his head to one side, examining her. "You want me to believe you didn't leave with him?"

He already believed she'd been his father's mistress. His bad opinion of her couldn't get any worse. "I don't care what you believe. But I'm telling you I went home alone." She brushed past him. "Goodness, you have a low opinion of me. First you accuse me of being your father's mistress, now I'm Xander's lover. Make up your mind!"

From behind her, he murmured, "Put like that it does sound a little excessive. I believe you that Xander is nothing more than a colleague."

"Gee, thanks."

"You don't have to leave, Jess. You can come back."

She swung around to face him, unable to believe what she was hearing. Before she could reply he'd pulled her into his arms. The dark turmoil had vanished from his expression, replaced by a primal intensity she recognised. Her heart quickened as he said, "Hush, don't say anything. Just think about this."

This turned out to be a kiss so hot, so passionate, that Jessica gasped as his lips slanted across hers. Instantly he pressed the advantage. His tongue swept into her mouth, tasting her like she was the sweetest thing in the world. He groaned and his arms tightened around her. Jessica was conscious of his height, of the hard wall of his chest, of his strength and her own femininity.

Then she became aware of the length of his erection pressing against her.

"No!" That was exactly what had landed her in the bind she was in. And she wasn't about to compound her mistake by landing back in Ryan Blackstone's bed.

He raised his head. "No?"

"I don't want this. I want to go home."

"*This* is your home, Jessica."

She wrenched herself out his arms. "This place? My home? Never!" His startled expression was almost comical. "Do you think that a million-dollar love-nest with great artwork—" she gestured to the abstract Fred Williams landscape on the wall "—and a professionally designed interior with fancy wooden floors and leather couches is what I would call home?" This was no space for a kid to grow up. "It's such a showplace, you didn't even want my cat here."

"Bring the damn cat then. If that's what it will take to make you happy."

"It's not about Picasso."

He frowned. "Then what *is* it about? You say that Xander's not the reason you left. Nor is your cat. So why did you go?"

Jessica drew a deep shuddering breath. "How can you ask

me that when you believe I could be your father's mistress while living with you?"

He held up a hand. "Wait, I've been thinking about that." For an instant a hint of vulnerability flashed in his eyes. "I got it wrong. I apologise."

"Thanks! And that's supposed to make me happy?" She glared at him, the hurt back in full force. How dare he have doubted her even for a minute? She sighed in frustration. "You turned my life upside down. An apology is not going to fix it. This is not like putting Humpty Dumpty back together again. You and me…it's not going to work, Ryan."

"Hang on." He looked so bewildered that she wanted to pummel him. "We were happy together."

He'd been happy. She'd have done anything to keep him happy. She shrugged. "It was all on your terms."

"I told you I didn't want marriage—"

"I'm not asking you to marry me," she interrupted before he could say anything more hurtful. "I don't even think marriage would make it right anymore." By his darkening eyes she knew that shocked him. "Since coming to Sydney I can't help noticing how much like your father you've become."

He narrowed his eyes. "You knew I wanted to be chairman of Blackstone's, that I wanted more, a bigger role in the company."

"How much more do you need? Surely you have enough wealth and power to keep you happy for your lifetime." She glanced at his set expression. "It doesn't matter, Ryan. This—us—was never going to last. It's better for it to end now." She sighed. "Are you going to help me pack or not?"

His lips drew into a flat, straight line. "You're making a mistake."

It would be a bigger mistake to stay. Ryan didn't want a baby, a family. And even if he asked her to stay after she told him that she was pregnant, how could she tie him down to a situation he'd been honest enough to tell her he never wanted? He'd come to resent her and the baby, and she wouldn't be able to bear that. She had no choice but to get out of his life. And later, when things had settled down a little, when she'd started to show and could no longer hide her pregnancy, then she'd tell him about the baby he didn't want.

It would be too late for him to demand that she abort their child.

There was an awkward moment when Ryan entered the showroom on Monday morning carrying a bulky black briefcase. His eyes met Jessica's across the vast space, and one look at his face told her that Ryan hadn't forgiven her for not crawling back into his bed when he crooked his little finger.

Jessica tensed, dreading the next round of recriminations, then spotted the woman dressed in a flowing, turquoise dress behind him, bracelets jangling on her slim arms. Iridescent opals arranged in flowers bloomed on a circlet of silver that nestled against her throat. She looked like Persephone, the goddess of spring.

Jessica gave her a smile, grateful for the reprieve from meeting Ryan alone after their last searing encounter.

"Jessica, you know my cousin Danielle, don't you?" Ryan asked, halting beside the row of chest-level display cases that served as a counter, and setting the briefcase down.

"We didn't meet at the funeral. But we've spoken on the phone." Jessica moved from behind the counter where she'd been giving Candy, one of the sales team, a set of instructions, and shook hands with his cousin. "I'm sorry for the loss your family suffered."

Sadness clouded Dani's eyes. "Mum and I miss him terribly."

Jessica resisted the unkind temptation to retort that many

didn't miss Howard Blackstone for a moment. Including herself. No, that would be unnecessarily cruel. And she wasn't sinking to Howard's level.

"Excuse me, I need to make a couple of calls," Ryan cut in. "I'll use your office, Jessica."

"Of course." *Their* office now, according to what he'd told her on Friday. It was going to be impossible to share that small space with such a big man. Jessica refused to run hungry eyes over Ryan's tall, broad frame. Reminding herself that she was mad at him, she kept her attention on Dani. "I've always called you Dani because that's the name you run your business under. Do you prefer Danielle?"

Dani grimaced. "To my family I'll always be Danielle. But in Port Douglas everyone knows me as Dani. They also know me dressed like this." She gestured ruefully to her colourful dress. "I'm flying back to Port Douglas straight after this, so don't tell my mother that I didn't wear a business suit to the store. She'd be embarrassed. And you can call me anything you want."

Jessica laughed, warming to Dani's refreshing candour. "My Mum has things she'd like me to do, too. Like find a nice man and get married."

"Mine, too." Dani grinned conspiratorially. Then she spotted the pile of brochures for the launch on the glass-topped counter. "Ooh, are any of my designs in here?"

"Take a look," Jessica invited. "The images of the designs you sent came out beautifully."

Dani Hammond was a breath of fresh summer air. Jessica couldn't help smiling at Dani's enthusiasm as she leafed through the pages, her eyes glowing with delight.

"Gosh, this stone is stunning. Imagine cutting that." Her tone held awe. "I'd be petrified at the thought of making the first cut."

Jessica peered over her shoulder. "Amazing, isn't it?

That's the Desert Star, the first of the big stones that came out the Janderra mine after it was first opened. It will be on display as part of the history of Blackstone's, but it's not for sale."

"My uncle showed it to me once when I was a little girl. He told me that it was flawless. Colourless. I remember the fire that flashed inside the heart of the stone and I told him that it couldn't possibly be called colourless. Not with all those sparkles."

"It's in the vault. Would you like to see it again?"

"Please!" Dani dropped the brochure and leapt forward, hoisting up the briefcase that Ryan had carried in. "I've brought some of my pieces for the show with me. They'll need to be put in the vault, too."

They made their way to the vault set behind the showroom. It had no windows, no natural lighting and the bright electric light shone starkly over the banks of metal-fronted drawers. Jessica unlocked a drawer, lifted out a box and flipped it open to reveal a solitary polished gem twinkling against black velvet.

"Let me see." Dani's voice held wonder. And for a moment Jessica could imagine the little girl she must once have been.

Jessica passed the box over. "It may not be a fancy coloured diamond like the most valuable stones mined at Janderra, but the colour and clarity are superb. Just over eleven carats, a D-colour, internally flawless cushion-shaped diamond. Hard to believe that much beauty is nothing more than atoms of carbon bonded together."

"Ooh, an old mine cut." Dani's eyes stretched wide. Her fingers touched the stone with reverence. "Howard was right. This stone is truly colourless. And the fire. The brilliance. Look at the symmetry, and how the light dances from facet to facet. It's a wonderful job. Aaron Lazar was a master cutter. I'm so envious of his talent." Dani looked up at Jessica.

"Lazar also cut the Heart of the Outback—the stone that my grandfather gave to Auntie Ursula and Uncle Howard just after James was born. He and Howard were business partners—that's how my Auntie Ursula met and married Howard."

"Ryan doesn't talk about his mother." Jessica couldn't resist probing for information. "I heard she committed suicide when he was little."

"He was only three when she died." Some of the radiance and sparkle drained from Dani's golden eyes.

Jessica half wished she'd never mentioned it.

"Mum says as a toddler Ryan used to stand by the gate, clutching the bars, waiting for his mother to one day come home. Once he understood that she'd died and gone to heaven, he used to ask the postman if there were any letters for him. He told Mum that even in heaven he was sure Ursula would remember to send him a postcard."

Jessica's heart cracked wide open for the lonely little boy he'd once been.

Then Dani seemed to give herself a mental shake. She looked round theatrically and whispered, "It's all part of the family scandal. The stuff we never talk about."

Did that mean Dani wasn't going to be any help in filling her in on the dark spaces in Ryan's life? Jessica took the hint and went back to the subject of diamonds. "I've heard about the Heart of the Outback. Over a hundred carats in the rough before Howard had Lazar cut it into five stones and assembled into a necklace called—"

"—the Blackstone Rose. Those five cut stones must have been stunning. Four of them were seven carats and the fifth, a pear-shaped stone, weighed almost ten carats." Dani shook her head. "No wonder my Uncle Oliver—that's my mum's brother—was mad as anything about it."

Jessica stilled, reluctant to interrupt lest Dani remember that she was talking to an outsider. And she was very much an outsider—despite her relationship to Ryan. Howard Blackstone had made that clear enough the last time she'd seen him. She would never be accepted into the Blackstone fold. She didn't have the right connections, the right pedigree that Howard wanted for the woman who married his son.

Dani perched herself on a waist-high steel safe that held a fortune in jewels. "That fancy pink diamond brought nothing but bad luck to our family. The necklace was stolen on the night of Ryan's mum's thirtieth birthday party." Dani gave a theatrical shudder. "And the fights and accusations haven't stopped since."

Jessica had read the speculation in the press about the events of that scandalous long-ago night. Knowing Howard, Jessica privately agreed with the notion that Howard had stolen the necklace himself to rip off the insurance company. Not that she'd ever admit that to anyone—especially not to Ryan. And the insurance company must've leaned that way, too, because they'd never paid out on the theft, much to Howard's reported rage. "The press had all sort of theories about who stole it."

Dani sighed. "It did horrible things to our family. You know, after that my Uncle Oliver never wanted to see my Mum or my Auntie Ursula again. He'd only come to the party because his wife begged him to come and put an end to the feud between himself and Howard. But instead of making things better, they only got worse after the necklace went missing. Not that Uncle Howard ever took it out on Mum or me. He was like a fairy godfather to me."

Howard Blackstone? A fairy godfather? Jessica gave Dani a sideways look of disbelief.

Dani intercepted it and tossed her head, and her coppery curls bobbed around her freckled face. "Is it that hard to believe Howard had a softer side?"

"Frankly, yes." Jessica thought of the overbearing, domineering man she'd grown to know.

"He was hard on Ryan and Kim. Perhaps it was different for me because he didn't have the same expectations for me. Or maybe he'd mellowed a little by the time I grew older. He did so much for me. He even loaned me money—interest free—to set up my business. Without Howard I'd still be backpacking around Asia, and I'd never have gotten the chance to pursue my dream of creating my own designs."

"Designs that will be a runaway success at the show at the end of the month." Jessica decided to change the subject. She'd never be able to be cool and rational about Howard.

Dani looked unaccustomedly nervous. "I hope you're right, Jessica."

"I am. Believe me on this. Dani Hammond is going to be the hottest name in town."

Dani gave a lopsided smile. "There's some kind of irony in that. A Blackstone event making a Hammond famous." Then all humour left her eyes. "I hate this stupid feud. At the funeral I wanted to go say hello to Matt Hammond. He's my cousin, after all. But he looked so hard and angry that it felt disloyal to Howard's memory, and I couldn't bring myself to do it."

Sadness seeped through Jessica. "I hate it, too. So many tensions." Between Ryan and Ric. Between Ryan and Matt Hammond. "Why can't it just end?"

"My mother says that Uncle Oliver fought with his father because he thought that the Heart of the Outback should have been his. Granddad gave it to Uncle Howard and my aunt Ursula when James was born. To celebrate. After James's kidnapping, Uncle Oliver said that it served Howard and Ursula right that their son had been taken. They'd stolen what was rightfully his, so the diamond put a curse on them."

How could anyone have been so cruel? Jessica knew she

would die if her child was taken from her. But perhaps it hadn't been so simple....

"I heard that Howard accused Oliver of kidnapping James," Jessica said.

"But it wasn't true—"

"Oliver Hammond stole the Blackstone Rose off his sister's—my mother's—neck." Ryan's harsh interruption made Jessica jump.

But he hadn't finished. "Like father, like son—now Matt Hammond is trying to steal Blackstone shares. What else could one expect from a Hammond?"

Her mortification at being caught gossiping was overtaken when Jessica caught the flash of hurt in Dani's eyes. *Damn.* Didn't Ryan realize that he'd hurt Dani with his bullheaded reaction against the Hammond name? "I thought you had some calls to make?" Jessica tried to stop him saying anything that might make matters worse.

Ryan's face was set, and his green eyes were colder than a frozen lake in winter.

"I own this store, remember?"

Jessica flushed at the pointed rebuke. She'd just been reminded of her place. He gave the orders. Not her. He was the boss.

Dani slid off the steel safe where she'd been perched. "I should go. I've got a plane to catch."

"Don't leave on my account, cousin."

Dani raised an eyebrow, flags of colour high on her cheeks. "I'm not sticking around if you're in a bad mood," she said with the candid familiarity of someone who had grown up in the family.

Ryan's face cracked into a smile. "Sorry! I always think of you as one of us. I forget that you have the misfortune of bearing the Hammond name."

"And Hammond blood beats in your heart, too," Dani retorted.

"Still as forthright as ever. I pity the man who tries to tame you, pumpkin."

Jessica envied the easy familiarity between the two of them. But his statement describing Dani as *one of us* only emphasised how much of an outsider she was. And how right she'd been to end the sorry excuse for a relationship that they had.

After Dani had gone, her hurt spilling over, Jessica turned on Ryan. "That was rude."

He looked startled. "What? Calling Dani 'pumpkin'?"

"Accusing the Hammonds of being nothing more than a pack of thieves."

"I was referring to Oliver Hammond and his son. Dani knows I don't mean her."

"Does she?" Jessica narrowed her gaze. "Or does she think you despise her, too?"

"She's my cousin, for Pete's sake." His tone grew heated. "As she pointed out, my mother was a Hammond so I'm half Hammond, too. But that doesn't change the fact that Oliver is nothing more than a liar, a cheat and a thief."

"He's your uncle *and* Dani's uncle. But Dani's still not a Blackstone, even though she grew up amongst you. In her position I'd feel torn in two."

"You would?"

"Yes! She's caught in the crossfire. Do you know she wanted to greet Matt at the funeral, but she was worried about being disloyal to Howard's memory?"

"That's commendable. Dani's always been a loyal little thing."

"But Howard is dead!" Jessica wanted to shake him. God, but he could be intransigent. "She and Matt are alive. He's her cousin. And yours, too. Don't you think it's time to bury the hatchet?"

"In Matt Hammond's head?"

Jessica threw her arms into the air. "I give up! I can't talk to you. You're the most stubborn—" She broke off. Why was she allowing herself to get all worked up? Jessica drew a deep breath. Turning away, she placed the sparkling Desert Star into its box with careful hands and put it back in the drawer. "Thankfully this has nothing to do with me. I only work here."

But even that was not permanent. Once the baby was born…

"Matt is out to destroy Blackstone's." Ryan had moved up right behind her. Jessica stopped breathing. "Everything my father and I—and even Ric," he added grudgingly, "have worked so hard to build is in jeopardy."

Something is his voice caught her attention and she swung around to face him. "Do you really believe Matt can damage Blackstone's?"

Ryan nodded, and his eyes glittered in the artificial light. "Yes, he can. Matt is out for revenge. At any cost."

"Do you think it's because—" She broke off.

"Because my father stole his wife?" Ryan shrugged. "I don't know. And I don't particularly care who my father's mistress was."

For a moment something flashed in the depths of his eyes as he looked at her. A hint of pain…or something else? Ryan must be hurting that his idol, his father, was proving to have feet of clay. But who knew what really went on behind that handsome face? It was entirely possible that he thought the speculation about Howard stealing Marise from Matt was a bunch of rot—because he'd already decided *she* was his father's mistress.

Then he growled, "But I'm not going to let Matt destroy Blackstone's."

Five

The emerald turf of Flemington racecourse provided a dramatic backdrop for the jewel-bright silks worn by the jockeys. In the parade ring, the best of this year's fillies circled. Some walked on a loose rein, while others snatched at the bit and kept breaking into a trot, showing high spirits.

"Beautiful, aren't they?"

At the sound of Ryan's rough voice, Jessica lowered the binoculars.

He was dressed entirely in black. A black suit, black shirt and highly polished black Italian shoes. He looked debonair, dangerous…and every inch a Blackstone. "I wasn't sure that you were coming."

She met his gaze squarely. "I certainly didn't expect to see you here. You said—"

"That I was going to Janderra?" The satisfaction in his voice alerted her.

He'd deliberately misled her!

Why? To ensure that she came to the races? Had he thought—correctly—she might back out if she'd known he would be in the Blackstone box today? Yes, that was it.

Seething, she lifted the binoculars.

"Which filly do you fancy?" he asked at her shoulder.

"I don't bet." It sounded so prim that Jessica almost groaned out aloud.

"I know that. But last year you picked the winner before the race had even started."

"I'm surprised you even noticed." In the past two years they'd barely looked at each other at the racetrack. Absolute discretion. No one could've guessed they were lovers.

"I notice everything about you," Ryan murmured softly. "I even remember that full skirted black dress you wore last year…and how I unlaced the tight corset top afterwards."

Jessica stifled a soft groan. She didn't want to remember how after the St. Valentine's Ball—after pretending to be nothing more than boss and employee—she and Ryan had gone back to the apartment the Blackstones maintained on the spacious top floor of a sought-after building. Or how they'd shared a bottle of Taittinger in the hot tub.

Those memories were far too seductive.

And nothing like that would happen tonight. Because tonight she would be staying in the five-star Ascot Gold Hotel. Alone.

A chestnut filly pranced past in front of them, sunlight burnishing the bunched muscle of her hindquarters. The jockey wore black silks with a large pink diamond emblazoned on the front and back. A Blackstone horse.

"What's that filly's name?"

"Diamond Lady." Ryan barely looked at the horse. "Do you remember how we spent the next day in bed? Only getting up for a meal in the evening?"

She'd been totally in his thrall.

"Jessica...Ryan!"

Jessica gave a start of surprise. She could've kissed Briana for the timely interruption. Wearing a stunning silk yellow dress that only a very confident woman could pull off, her golden-brown hair artfully curled around her face, Briana walked beside a tall, dark-haired stranger.

"Jake Vance," Briana announced. "Jake, meet Ryan Blackstone...and my friend, Jessica, who manages the big Sydney Blackstone's store."

Jake's smile was wide and white. She'd heard the name before but Jessica couldn't remember where. Had Briana found comfort in her time of loss? Jessica sincerely hoped so.

"Are you ready to go up to the seating enclosure?" Briana asked.

"Yes," Jessica responded hastily. The company would dilute Ryan's attention.

"So, Jess, who do you favour to win the Blackstone stakes?" Jake Vance asked.

"Diamond Lady." Jessica didn't miss a beat.

Both Briana and Jake laughed.

"I should've expected that," Jake said wryly.

"I'm going to place a bet on that filly." Ryan started to move away.

"Not on my opinion, I hope," Jessica said in alarm. She'd simply repeated the name she'd heard seconds before. "There's no scientific basis to my choice."

"Maybe it's a woman's intuition," Briana mused. "I think I'll put a bet on Diamond Lady."

"Then I'd better, too," Jake added.

Jessica dropped her head into her hands. "Don't blame me when you all lose your hard-earned cash," she called after them and made her way to the Blackstone seating enclosure.

Five minutes later the other three arrived. "Jess, my bet didn't even break the bank." Briana dropped into the seat beside her.

Jessica met her friend's smiling eyes. "It's good to see you here, sweetie," she said softly. "And I'm so glad to see you with someone other than Patrick."

Briana waved a dismissive hand. "Jake and I aren't serious. I needed to get out and Jake invited me. That's all."

"Maybe it will develop into something special."

"Oh, you…romantic!" Briana laughed. "We need to find you a guy. You haven't dated in the all the time I've known you."

"I'm trying to talk Jess into going to dinner with me tonight." Ryan approached holding two tall tulip glasses filled with champagne.

"Thank you," Briana took one. Then she turned to Jessica. "Oh, Jess, you can't refuse an invitation like that!"

Jessica shot Ryan a killing look. *Wanna bet?* "You can't take me to dinner. You need to make an appearance at the St. Valentine's Ball after the races—and I don't have a ticket," she said with quiet triumph. She'd refused the offer of a ticket to the ball back in Sydney, intending to have an early night.

"You can be my partner." Ryan grinned at her.

What was he doing?

Before Jessica could object, Briana smiled and said, "That's settled! Why don't the four of us sit together tonight?"

Great. Now Briana thought she'd matched the couple of the century. Jessica wanted to brain Ryan. Instead she made do with looking away and ignoring him. After years of secrecy, now that their affair was over he wanted everyone to know they were a couple? It didn't make sense.

But she didn't have to go. "It's black tie—and I haven't brought a suitable dress along." All she had was the white linen suit she was wearing. Dressed up with a stylish black

at and a silver camisole and her familiar pearls, it was smart
enough for the races but nowhere near formal enough for the
ball. Last year she'd worn a floor-length lace dress in the
palest shade of aqua.

"That's easy to fix," Briana declared. "I have a deal with
a couple of designers to show off their clothes. They'd have
no problem with dressing you." Briana already had her cell
phone in her hand. A moment later she was speaking to
someone with the unlikely name of ZinZin.

Jessica glared at Ryan. He lifted his glass in a silent toast.
What had he gotten her into? And why now, of all times? The
very last thing she wanted was to be seen out in public with
him and have people adding two and two and coming up with
pregnant when she started to show in a few weeks' time.

"That's settled. Cinderella can go to the ball," Briana said
with some satisfaction as she ended the call.

Jessica bit back an acid comment. She would go to the ball
as Ryan's partner. It would be worth it to keep that smile back
on Briana's beautiful face.

"Oh, the horses are off!" Briana got to her feet.

A thrill surged through Jessica and her irritation with Ryan
was forgotten.

"Sorry." Briana sat down, laughing, too. "But it's always
so exciting when the horses leap out onto the track."

"Even a hardened businessman like me finds it exciting."
Jake winked at Briana.

Was it serious? Despite Briana's denials Jessica hoped so.
Briana deserved some happiness after her abortive previous
relationship. Jessica had never cared much for Patrick—too
smooth. Too charming. Jake, on the other hand, looked tough
and ruthless. Jessica frowned as she tried to remember where
she'd heard his name. Briana didn't need more hurt after the
tough time she'd had recently.

"Here they come!" Ryan's exclamation had her leaning forward to squint at the horses in the lead bunch. "And Diamond Lady is right up there."

The fillies thundered past the stands, the jockeys bent over their necks, their bodies in rhythm with the horseflesh beneath them. The roar of the crowd was deafening.

"She might make it!"

The excitement in Ryan's voice was contagious. Jessica grabbed his hand, squeezing it tightly as the horses flashed past the finish line. The sight of the chestnut filly and the jockey's pink and black colours magnified on the huge television screen on the opposite side of the track led to loud whoops.

Briana swung to her, a delighted smile on face. "See? I didn't lose a cent."

"Yes!" Ryan punched the air.

"Diamond Lady won!" Jessica couldn't believe it. Without realising it, she found herself on her feet, jumping up and down in delight.

Ryan pulled her into his arms, hugging her, his face blazing with triumph. And then he kissed her.

It was a quick kiss, full of elation and joy. But their eyes caught and held.

Hurriedly, Jessica said, "Shouldn't you be down in the winner's enclosure to present the trophy?"

Ryan dropped his arms and stepped back. "Kim's doing the family honours this year. I've done it all the years she's been away in New Zealand. Ric's down there with her."

A pang of disappointment pierced her as he moved away. It seemed like aeons since she'd last touched him.

"Besides," Ryan continued, "it's much nicer up here in the box, sipping French champagne and sitting with you. Can I top up your glass?"

Jessica set her glass down. "I've had enough. I still have to drive back to my hotel and get ready for the ball."

Then Briana was saying, "Where are you staying, Jess? I'll have ZinZin send over a selection of dresses for you to try on."

"The Ascot Gold Hotel." For a mad moment Jessica wished she knew what Ryan had been thinking when he looked at her with that strange intensity.

"I'll meet you in the lobby at seven." Something glinted in the depths of Ryan's green eyes.

The dress that Jessica had chosen from the selection ZinZin sent over was soft and feminine. The wraparound style made her confident that the thickening waist only she knew about didn't show.

A soft mix of palest apricot and rich creams, the gown hung to the floor in fine pleats and emphasized the lustrous glow of her skin. She'd put her hair up. A pair of flawless diamond studs that Ryan had given her last Christmas twinkled in her ears. She knew she looked good. Picking up a small sequined bag and the pashmina wrap that ZinZin had matched with the dress, Jessica made for the door.

Downstairs, Ryan was waiting for her, wearing a white dinner jacket and a black bow tie.

For an instant his sheer male beauty took Jessica's breath away and she stilled, then she moved forward. "I hope I didn't keep you waiting."

"No. I'm staying in the hotel as well."

"Here? At the Ascot?"

Ryan nodded. "Kim and Ric are staying at the apartment. There's really not enough space for me there, too."

Jessica could imagine that Kim and Ric's renewed closeness might cause Ryan to feel like a spare part. While the apartment was undeniably luxurious, it was a lover's retreat.

Jessica had wondered in the past if Howard Blackstone had bought it as a lover's nest to share with his latest "secretary."

"You're staying here because of the ball?" It was highly unlikely that Ryan had chosen to stay here because of her, Jessica told herself. Ryan couldn't have known—or cared— where she was staying.

His gaze shifted away. He held out an arm. "Come, we don't want to be the last to arrive."

And thereby attracting even more speculation than their arrival together already would.

The St. Valentine's Diamond Ball was held in the ballroom of the Ascot, a vast room lit with dozens of brilliant chandeliers. Silver cutlery glittered on the round tables, which were covered with snowy white tablecloths and adorned with sprays of ivy and tall elegant white candles.

They made their way to the main Blackstone table where Kim and Ric, Briana and Jake and a host of familiar faces from the Melbourne Blackstone's Jewellery store were already seated.

After greeting them, Briana said, "That dress looks stunning, Jess. I knew ZinZin would find something perfect for you."

"It was perfect advice."

"You look almost—" Briana paused "—voluptuous tonight."

Jessica gave a self-conscious little laugh. But apprehension stirred. She couldn't afford for Briana to guess....

"I guess I've picked up a little bit of weight lately."

"It suits you." Briana's eyes scanned her face. "You're glowing."

"I noticed that, too." Ryan leant forward. "You're growing more beautiful every day, Jess."

Even Briana looked startled by this observation.

"Flatterer," Jessica exclaimed quickly, and resisted the urge to place her hands over the barely noticeable curve of her stomach hidden by the artful pleats of the soft fabric.

"You're not talking about Ryan, are you?" Kim entered the conversation. "My brother never wastes time on flattery. What did he say?"

"Never mind." Jessica could feel herself flushing.

Kim's gaze grew knowing. Jessica grew even hotter. "Can we change the subject please?" she begged.

Kim came to her rescue. "I hear you predicted Diamond Lady's win today. I hope you had good odds on her."

"Um…I didn't bet." Jessica latched gratefully onto the change of subject.

"But everyone else did," Ryan added, and gave her a slow smile that caused tingles to run up and down Jessica's spine. She looked away hastily.

Briana instantly piped up about her winnings and Jake added that he'd been lucky enough to predict the trifecta. Then Briana passed a comment about financial sharks that suddenly set a lightbulb off in Jessica's head.

Jake Vance…financial shark. Corporate raider. Of course! How could she have forgotten a name that so often appeared in the financial pages.

During dinner the lively debate about horses and predicting winners continued. Jessica didn't contribute much—she was too aware of the man seated at her side.

When Ryan's chair scraped back, she gave an inward sigh of relief. No doubt he intended to circulate. She would have a reprieve from his overwhelming presence for a little while.

"Dance?"

Ryan stood beside her chair, his hand outstretched. Did she really have a choice? Reluctantly Jessica rose to her feet.

On the dance floor he gathered her close. She intercepted some speculative glances from several of the surrounding couples.

"We shouldn't be doing this."

Ryan's brows drew together. "Why not?"

"Everyone will think we're a couple."

Ryan's response was to draw her closer still. "Maybe we should be."

"No!" That couldn't happen. "It's too late for that. I don't want people to think—"

"I don't particularly care what they think."

That was Ryan. Arrogant. Outspoken. And then he blew her preconceptions away by saying, "I want you to be happy. So if it makes you unhappy to be this close to me, just say the word and I'll let you go."

"Let me go?" She looked up into his face. "You mean you'd stop dancing and return me to the others?"

"If that's what you want."

He would, too. She heard the resolve in his voice. And he'd probably never ask her to dance again. Then she'd never be held this close to him again. Jessica didn't know if she could bear that.

So instead of pulling away, she stayed in his arms, so close that she could feel the steady beat of his heart against her cheek. The moment to back away was gone.

"You smell so good," he murmured, nuzzling her hair. His fingers trailed across her back. "You feel so good."

Little shivers shook her. Had he missed her? It would be too much to hope for.

Even if he had, what would change? Ryan had no desire for a wife or a family. The high-flying corporate executive life he led was a world away from what Jessica had realised over the past six weeks she wanted. A family home, a man with time to spend with her—to watch their child grow up. She didn't want a man who was driven by power and profit. If the truth be told, deep in her secret heart, she wanted a man who loved her more than anything in the world.

And that man could never be Ryan.

Yet she fit against the hard angles of his body as though she'd been made for him. And as he shifted to the music her body swayed with him. That tantalising hand slid down her back, to rest on her hips and waves of dizzying longing swept her.

She'd missed this closeness.

She missed lying curled against him in the dead of the night. She missed hearing his husky voice saying her name. She missed seeing him seated across the breakfast table from her. She missed *him*.

Without thinking about it, she snuggled closer. Ryan's arms tightened and his cheek moved against her hair. The warmth of his body and a subtle hint of the expensive after-shave he wore surrounded her.

When the song came to an end, he held her for a heartbeat past the end. Then he let her go.

A wild emptiness filled her. She stood an arm's length away from him and it felt as if he were a world away.

Jessica shivered again as loneliness sliced through her.

"Come." His arm came around her shoulders and he guided her back to the table where Ric and Kim sat, their faces close together, totally absorbed in each other.

Ryan picked up her evening bag and her pashmina. "I'm taking Jessica home," he declared. "Say our farewells to Briana and Jake."

Kim looked startled, then she smiled.

Jessica thought about objecting to Ryan's high-handed-ness. But one look into his smouldering eyes and the flash of rebellion subsided.

Once they left the ballroom, the music dimmed and Jessica became aware of the simmering silence between them. It deepened as they entered the elevator. Ryan's index finger hovered over the control panel. "Which floor are you on?" His voice was rough.

She told him.

The silence returned. A living, breathing force that pushed them apart. Jessica stared at the red digital numbers flashing as they passed by each floor. When the elevator stopped and the doors opened, she bolted out.

"I'll see you to your room."

"It's not necessary," she said in a strangled voice, not daring to look at him. But he paid no heed and strode beside her down the carpeted corridor.

Jessica was aware of every muffled step it took them to reach her room. She could feel herself becoming more breathless with each passing second.

She halted and fumbled in her bag for the access card, conscious of her chest rising and falling.

"Invite me in, Jess."

She looked at him then. In the muted light of the corridor she glimpsed heat in his eyes…and the same tension that filled her lonely heart.

She knew what she wanted.

"Yes," she whispered and his eyes flared until they became as dark and unfathomable as midnight.

"Good," he purred, then took the card from her nerveless fingers and swiped it. The door clicked open, the sound overloud in the night.

He pushed the door open and Jessica stepped through into the bedroom beyond.

Six

"Come to me, Jess."

Ryan stood beside the bed, his features stark with want.

"I can't." Paralysed with fear that if she let him touch her, she might never again find the strength to leave, Jessica folded her arms tightly across her chest and watched as Ryan approached. The glaring overhead light fell across his face, highlighting the taut cheekbones and turning his eyes to blazing emerald.

"Meet me halfway, then. For tonight."

One night…

"Only for tonight?"

He hesitated, then nodded, a swift jerky movement.

She could do one night, couldn't she? Jessica took a step forward. Then another. Before she knew it she was in his arms.

His hands pressed her against him, uncompromising. The pashmina slipped to the floor, and his hands confidently stroked the naked skin that the low-cut back left exposed. But instead of resisting, instead of resenting his demonstration of dominance, desire exploded through her. She made a little keening noise in the back of her throat.

His lips came down on the side of her throat, under her jaw, and she tipped her head back and muttered incoherent sounds of desire. The mouth that closed over hers was hard and hungry and she responded with an alien, unladylike wildness she'd never shown before.

He groaned and his fingers dug into her upper arms. "God, this is happening much faster than I expected."

His hips surged forward and Jessica was conscious of his hardness pressing into her, conscious of the life that lay in her womb where he'd already impregnated her. The knowledge was strangely erotic.

But it reminded her that she wasn't as reed slim as the last time she'd been in his bed.

"The lights," she whimpered. "Turn the lights off."

"I want to see you. I want to feast my eyes on every naked morsel of your flesh."

She shuddered. "No."

He pulled away, staring down into her eyes. Into her soul. "Why the sudden shyness, Jess?"

"I'm not shy." She buried her face in his shoulder, the fabric of his jacket hiding her expression. "But I don't want you to see me."

"But I've seen every inch of you before." The tension threaded through his voice subsided a little, replaced by gentle amusement.

Her heart contracted. "But tonight is…different."

"How?"

"Because…" *What to say?* She certainly couldn't tell him about the fuller curves that she didn't want him to see.

"Because we're not really together anymore." She writhed at the deception. But if she told him…

That would be the end.

No cats. No kids. No press. No diamond rings.

He would walk out the door. She'd hear from his lawyers. It would soon be too late for the suggestion of a face-saving abortion—her greatest fear, given the wealth and power of the Blackstones. Yet she was confident that Ryan wouldn't walk away from his financial responsibility. He'd send her a maintenance cheque for the child every month. But he would never touch her again.

And she'd missed his touch.

He might not love her but he still wanted her with the same hunger that had always raged between them. For tonight—for only one night—she would be his. And he would be hers. It would have to be enough.

He released her. She felt cold. Then the room plunged into darkness.

"Okay, if I'm not allowed to see you, I'll touch you. I'll remember every bit of your skin with my fingertips."

The husky, evocative words caused her breath to quicken. His fingers touched her cheek in the darkness, warming her, driving out the chill. One finger traced her cheekbone, before they all speared into her hair, pushing out the pins. She felt the soft locks fall around her face.

Shivers of desire shook her, growing with every passing second. The sensation swept through her, heating her blood, heightening her anticipation.

His other hand cupped her jaw, tilting her face up. Then his lips touched hers in the darkness, ever so gently, with light, unsatisfying kisses that teased as much as they provoked. Her lips parted, inviting him in. Wanting more… wanting him.

But instead of deepening the kiss, he let his tongue trace her lips, driving her wild.

She wanted more.

More pressure.

More passion.

And a thousand times more pleasure than the tender butterfly touches gave her.

"Kiss me," she whispered impatiently against his mouth.

He lifted his head. "I am."

"Kiss me properly."

He stilled. "Why don't you show me how you want to be kissed?"

Jessica hesitated. If she kissed him, he'd know exactly how much she still wanted him. So what? Desiring him wouldn't mean revealing her other secrets. Like how much she loved him. And how much she missed him. Nor would he find out about the baby.

So long as the lights stayed off.

So why the hell not? She'd show him how she wanted to be kissed. Properly. Or maybe not so properly. Maybe tonight was the time for a little improper behaviour. Tonight she'd be the woman she never would have dared to be in the past.

She had nothing to lose.

"Okay." Her voice sounded husky, unfamiliar. "But first this needs to go." She slipped her hands inside his white dinner jacket and pushed it from his shoulders.

"Whatever you want." It was a rough whisper.

The fabric rustled. Jessica's arms circled his waist and deftly caught the jacket as it slid off his shoulders. She tossed it in the direction of the armchair she'd seen earlier and heard it land with a soft plop. She ran her hands up and down his back, loving the feel of the hard ridges of muscle either side of his spine under the sleek silk of his shirt.

His body vibrated with tension. "Now are you going to kiss me?"

"Wait."

He gave a theatrically loud sigh.

She brought her hands back to the front, so that she was no longer touching him. "Do you want me to stop?"

He groaned. "Jess, don't tease!"

"Tease?" She smiled into the darkness. "*This* is teasing?"

Feeling ahead of her, she stopped when the fabric of his shirt touched her fingertips. Careful not to brush his skin with her fingers, she lifted his silk dress shirt away from his body and tugged the snaps undone.

This time his groan was louder. "You're killing me."

Quickly Jessica yanked the shirt out of his pants and attacked the bottom snaps.

"Kiss me. Touch me, dammit."

"Your wish is thy mistress's command, oh Master." With great deliberation, she snaked her fingers up his bare chest, ignoring his harsh intake of breath, until she reached the last of the remaining snaps. She hunted for his bow tie and tugged it loose. An instant later she dealt with the final snaps.

The shirt fell to the ground with a faint whisper of sound.

Next her fingers tangled with the buttons of his fly. She released him and peeled his briefs off. He was trembling, shaking under the brush of her fingers, his body wired with tension.

"Come here." His voice was thick with desire, his arms closing around her and pulling her back onto the bed with him. "My turn to undress you."

"Do you remember the headboard?" she whispered to him. "There's a wooden rail across the top. I want you to hold on and not let go."

"Hey," he objected, "the deal was I couldn't see but my hands would be my eyes. I want to touch you all over."

That was what was worrying her. That he might find curves where previously there had been none.

"Hold the bar," she whispered, more insistent now.

He groaned. "And you mock me by calling me 'Master'?" But she heard him shift to grab the rail.

Jessica smiled slowly into the blackness. "I'm finding it's nice to be in control for a change." She straddled him and warned, "Don't move your hands."

"I want to see this." He flicked on the bedside light. The dull gold light bathed the room. Then he reached for the rail again.

"Aren't you going to take off that dress?"

"No!" Her gaze flickered to the lamp. Then she abandoned her anxiety and gave him a slow smile. "I've never made love to you fully clothed. And this dress is so beautiful, it makes me feel like Cinderella." *Just for tonight.*

"From where I'm lying, it's as sexy as hell."

She stroked him slowly, running her hands over his smooth golden skin until he writhed under her touch. But he didn't let go. There was something utterly compelling about having him stretched out on her bed, naked, while she, fully dressed, touched him to her heart's content.

Finally, when his breathing was ragged, she remained poised above him and then sank down. His hardness slid into the softness of her body, his heat warming her.

The feeling was incredible. Jessica found that she was already so wildly turned on by a combination of abstinence, hormones and Ryan's hard, naked body between her thighs.

She rose and sank again, until Ryan was panting out loud. "I can't hold on anymore."

Before she could protest, he'd let go of the rail and grabbed her hips, yanking her to him, then one arm came round her and pulled her down, so that her breasts brushed against his torso. "I want you closer." His voice was hoarse. "Damn, this is good."

And then they were both shuddering and pleasure streaked through Jessica in sharp electric bursts. For a moment she was shocked at her wildness, at the wanton way she'd taken charge.

There had been something curiously liberating about playing the mistress, teasing him and watching him lose total control.

Even if it was only for one night.

Dressed in last night's clothes, Ryan drew open the long curtains covering the floor-to-ceiling windows that overlooked the city. In the east, splashes of gold and a rosy pink signalled the dawn of another day. He turned back to the woman lying in the hotel bed. Sometime after he'd fallen asleep she'd changed out of her dress and slipped on a nightie.

She'd kicked off the covers and the nightie had ridden up, revealing long, bare tanned legs.

Those legs had been locked around his waist last night. Ryan shut his eyes and resisted the urge to sit down on the edge of the bed and stroke those long limbs.

The last time she'd lain in his bed had been the day of his father's funeral. By nightfall she'd been gone, driven away by his accusation that she was his father's lover.

Deep down, he no longer believed that. But he couldn't understand why she hadn't simply denied it.

Ryan's brows drew together. Her denial would have taken his doubts away in an instant. He would have believed her. Instead she'd walked away—and he'd been shocked at how much her leaving had devastated him.

He wanted her back.

Last night was another step in his careful campaign, and he'd gotten much more than he'd bargained for. At the memory of the wild night he started to harden. He considered waking her and indulging again.

Ryan's frown deepened at the sight of the digital clock on the bedstand. No time. He still needed to get back to his room for a shower and change of clothes, then he had to leave. Kimberley and Ric would be waiting for him at the airport. They'd arranged to fly to Sydney together in time for the weekly financial meeting.

Pale pink light filtered through the window, casting a rosy glow on Jessica's sleeping features. She looked so innocent, wholly at peace. Then he caught sight of the dress draped over the bottom of the bed—the innocent-looking dress that had transformed her into a wicked seductress last night.

For a moment he was tempted to give in to the urge to climb back into bed, to pull her into his arms, and forget about work, about Blackstone's.

Hell, how could he even be thinking that? After all the years he'd striven to get where he was? He sucked in a shaky breath.

Ric and Kimberley were waiting for him.

The snippet of conversation that was lodged in the forefront of his mind replayed itself again. He could hear Jessica's voice. "We shouldn't be doing this."

And his own response, "Why not?"

She'd stiffened in his arms and he'd heard her resistance. "Everyone will think we're a couple."

He'd responded by holding her tighter, knowing that she was slipping away from him. "Maybe we should be."

"No!" Jessica's answer had been very final. "It's too late for that."

He suspected that, unlike him, Jessica was going to regret the night they'd shared when she woke.

Resisting the urge to kiss her goodbye, he let himself quietly out of the room.

Before she awoke and he read regret in her eyes.

* * *

Jessica opened her eyes and blinked at the flood of bright February sunshine that streamed through the open curtains. The room was quiet. No water splashed. No electric razor buzzed. Nothing moved.

"Ryan?" Her voice echoed emptily through the hotel room and the adjoining bathroom. No answer. Her body slumped.

Ryan had gone.

She was alone again.

Dragging herself out the bed, she made her way to the dressing table. No message waited for her. She tried the empty surface beside the television. Nothing there. And nothing on the coffee table.

Her heart hollow, she made for the shower and turned the jets on full. After a few minutes of standing like a zombie, she washed and hauled herself out again.

Back in the room, Jessica reached for the first thing that came to hand from her suitcase—a pair of dark chocolate-coloured trousers. She pulled them on and added a filmy top with bold lime and taupe and white geometric patterns. Damp hair slicked back from her face, she quickly shoved the balance of her clothes into her bag. She was ready to go.

Downstairs at the checkout desk a queue of business folk waited to check out, briefcases at their feet, chatting among themselves. A pile of Melbourne morning newspapers lay in a stack beside a tray filled with small glasses of complimentary orange juice. Jessica helped herself to the juice and gulped it down. Setting down the empty glass, she picked up a paper and flipped through it. She reached the lifestyle supplement and found herself staring into her own laughing face.

Ryan's Racetrack Romance. She glared at the headline. Then at her photo. Idiot! Why had she been grinning up at

Ryan like a love-struck fool? Hardly surprising that the society reporter had gotten her facts wrong.

This was just what she didn't need. She hoped that no one who knew her would see it. But there was little chance of that.

Briana lived in Melbourne. Then there were the people who worked at the Melbourne Blackstone store. A few designers she worked with lived in the city.

Oh, dear! When she started showing and the news broke that she was pregnant, how many would put two and two together and come up with "Ryan's baby"? She could only pray for a reprieve.

A quick skim through the rest of the text revealed lots of speculation about her and the fact that she worked for Ryan. Howard Blackstone's recent death and the shocks contained in his will were rehashed. The reporter laboured over the fact that Ryan had lost Miramare. And down at the bottom of the article there was a faded colour photo of James, Ryan and their mother holding baby Kimberley outside Miramare.

Ryan would hate that.

Of course there was also a rundown of the previous women Ryan had dated—most of them daughters of Howard's golf club cronies. No surprises there. Then there was a snarky comment about his single state for the last two years.

If they only knew…

Jessica was even less pleased when she took in the inset photo showing him attending an event at the National Gallery of Victoria in St Kilda Road earlier in the year, a redhead plastered to his side wearing a skimpy dress and a wide smile.

Jessica frowned. She remembered that weekend. Ryan had gone to Melbourne on business. He'd mentioned the exhibition…but she'd assumed that he'd gone alone. She accepted that he had his own friends, his own social life. But *this*—she glared at the redhead—was not what they'd agr—

"Miss?" Jessica jerked around. The reception clerk was staring at her. No one stood in the queue ahead of her.

"Sorry." She grabbed her bag and rushed forward. "Name is Jessica Cotter." She handed over her access card. "I'd like to settle my bill and check out."

The keyboard tapped. The printer whirred. The reception clerk pulled out the bill and handed it to Jessica. "The account is already settled."

"There must be some mistake…" Jessica scanned the bill. Definitely all paid.

"It was paid a little over an hour ago," the clerk said helpfully. *Ryan.* Damn him, she could've settled it herself.

"And there's a message for you, Ms Cotter." The clerk handed her an envelope. Jessica moved to one side of the counter and slit it open with her index finger.

The note said:

Thanks for a sensational night. Had to leave for a meeting. See you at work.

He'd scrawled his name at the bottom and added:

P.S. Have that wicked dress charged to my account. I want you to think of me every time you see it or wear it.

Anger surged inside her, and all over again, she felt like a mistress. Nothing more than a night of passion. Unimportant. Paid for and discarded.

Her own stupid fault.

She'd played into the fantasy too well last night. Of course Ryan would regard her as nothing more than a mistress.

* * *

By the time Ryan sauntered into the first-floor showroom of Blackstone's, it was nearly midday and he hoped that Jessica would not read the fury of emotions stewing under his confident exterior.

He was eager to see her again. Yet he hardly knew how she would react. Would she want to turn their one night into more nights? Or would she regret the night they had shared?

Ryan searched for Jessica and found her pale blonde head shining like a beacon on the other side of the showroom, where she was helping a young couple. As Ryan drew nearer he saw that they were studying rings.

Diamond rings. Ryan hesitated. He heard her say, "What about narrowing it down to four or five that you like?"

"That will be hard," the young woman said. "They're all so beautiful. How would you choose?"

"I'd look for what fits with my personal style." Jessica drew a tray out from the locked drawers beneath the counter where some of the more valuable pieces were kept, in case any of Blackstone's favourite customers arrived without an appointment. "See this ring? It's a superb stone. But it's not ostentatious. I see a lot of very fine diamonds, but for me this one is special. I love the pale pink colour, the simplicity of the cut—it's an emerald cut, which is unusual for a coloured diamond. I like things very plain. It suits my style."

"That's an idea," the young woman said enthusiastically. She glanced at the man at her side. "Colin, let's each pick out a ring that appeals to us and see if we can find any that we both like."

"We want a stone that will be an investment. That's why we came to Blackstone's," said Colin, looking longingly at the ring that Jessica had pointed out. Ryan suspected it was the size of the stone that he liked, rather than the cut and style of the ring.

"I like that one." The woman pointed to a stone in an unusual shade of rich gold, set in a wide band with a design resembling leaves etched into the gold band. It was startlingly modern, very feminine and very different from the rest of the rings on the tray. "I love the warmth, the fire."

"A good choice," Jessica said, nodding in approval. "It's designed by one of our new designers, Dani Hammond. People will be killing for her designs after the launch of her new collection later this month."

"Does that mean the value will go up?"

"Oh, Colin." The young woman swatted her partner's arm and laughed. "Excuse him, he's a typical accountant, everything comes down to value. I won't be selling the ring, so it doesn't matter."

"Petra, the stone is not that big. With diamonds size really does matter."

"Carats aren't the only consideration." Ryan stepped forward. "There are other considerations."

"Like what?" Colin swivelled, clearly welcoming a male perspective.

"Cut. Dani Hammond is a top-class craftswoman. This gem has a unique facet pattern, she has used two different cuts, which shows off the reflected light brilliantly."

"It's different," Petra said. "That's what I love about it."

"And what else?" Colin asked Ryan, clearly not convinced yet.

"Clarity. And finally there's colour."

"Blue whites," said the young accountant. "That's what to buy. I was told to stay far away from brown diamonds. They're less valuable—and once cut they can turn orange or gold, so that they don't even look like brown diamonds." He cast a suspicious glance at the ring that Petra had admired.

"Yes," agreed Ryan. "But even brown can be beautiful."

He searched Jessica's startled gaze. "Some browns have warmth and glow with inner fire." A tinge of colour crept up under Jessica's fine-grained skin. She glanced down, her lashes dark against her cheeks. Ryan turned his attention back to the ring that Petra held. "That stone comes from Janderra, a mine deep in the outback Kimberley region. Janderra is famous for the candy-coloured stones it produces. Because of the intensity of the colour, that stone will be particularly rare. The rich deep yellow is unusual. It will always be a talking point."

The accountant started to look a little more interested. "Won't everyone think it is only a topaz?"

Jessica lifted the ring off Petra's palm and tipped it back and forth. "Topaz? With that inner fire? I think not. Look at the way it flashes and reflects the light."

"Is that what you really want, darling?"

Petra nodded enthusiastically. "It's beautiful."

"You'll be wearing it every day of your life, so it's important that you love it."

She stood on tiptoe. "What's important is that I love you and you love me." Their lips met.

The emptiness returned like a kick in the stomach. Ryan glanced at Jessica to see what she was thinking. But she was looking down, fiddling with the jeweller's trays. For an instant he felt devastatingly envious of the young couple, so secure, so in love.

Then he thrust the feeling aside.

Seven

Ryan couldn't help noticing Jessica's pensive expression as she watched the couple walking away, their fingers linked, the stunning yellow diamond ring firmly on Petra's left hand.

Despite her apparent happiness with the arrangement they'd had, and her denials that she didn't want marriage from him, did Jessica long to wear a diamond ring on her left finger?

"What are you thinking?" he asked.

"Moments like that are the highlights of my job. Two people, brave enough to give life together a go, who come into Blackstone's looking for a permanent symbol of their love."

"Jessica—" Ryan broke off.

She smiled up at him, a sweet curve of pale pink lips that he'd kissed to death last night. But her eyes held a wary light. "Yes?"

"About last night—"

"Last night was one night. Only one night. That's what we agreed." She turned away, locked the display counter and flicked a nonexistent fleck of dust off the top of the glass.

Clearly she didn't want to talk about the experience that had been utterly mind-blowing for him. He suppressed the disappointment that blasted through him. "It was. But I've been thinking—"

"Ryan, what are you doing here?"

Ryan bit back a curse as his sister's surprised voice sounded behind him.

"I thought you, Garth and Uncle Vincent were flying up to Janderra today?"

He turned to face his sister. "We postponed the trip. With the launch so close I decided it's better to stay close to Sydney." Near Jessica.

Kim glanced at him. Then back at Jessica. "I see."

Ryan frowned at his sister—a pointed sibling frown aimed at separating her from her erroneous conclusion as quickly as possible. She simply raised her eyebrows at him.

Despite whatever Kim's pensive green eyes saw, according to Jessica, he and she were finished. They'd had their one night.

"Holly can't join us for lunch, I'm afraid," Kimberley said to Jessica. "But I'll take notes of anything she needs to know."

"You two are having a lunch meeting?" Ryan asked.

Kimberley nodded. "At Flavio's across the road, to go over the final arrangements for the jewellery showing, before Monday morning's breakfast meeting with the event coordinator."

"I know about that," Ryan said. "I'm diarised to attend."

"Be warned." Kimberley gave him an evil grin. "If you attend Monday's meeting, I'll be spending some time talking to the coordinator about the ceremony Ric and I are having to renew our vows."

Ryan gave an exaggerated sigh. "Best thing I ever did was move down here. Head office was starting to feel like a bridal shower. Now let me get my jacket, and join you ladies for lunch. It sounds like I need to be there if it's about the show."

Kimberley narrowed her eyes, giving him a sly little look of amusement from under her lashes. But Ryan couldn't help noticing that Jessica didn't look nearly as amused.

Flavio's was smart and fashionable, the walls washed with an ochre shade reminiscent of a Tuscan villa. The wooden refractory-style tables were dark and narrow, and large oil paintings of village scenes hung on the walls. When the waiter came, Jessica ordered linguine Alfredo. The morning sickness had subsided at last, and she had acquired the appetite of a sumo wrestler. Kim elected to have grilled barramundi that the blackboard on the wall promised had been freshly flown in from Queensland.

While Ryan scrutinized the wine list, Jessica ordered a cola and thanked the heavens that she didn't often drink alcohol. Ryan had no reason to raise an eyebrow at her abstinence.

"And a bottle of Saxon's sauvignon blanc, please," Ryan said. After the waiter had departed, he turned to his sister. "I have it on best authority that the sauvignon blanc tastes of grapefruit, a hint of melon and a whole lot of summer."

"That sounds like it came from the mouth of a PR expert." Kimberley laughed. "Megan perhaps?"

Ryan nodded. "Spot on, sister. More cousins," he explained to Jessica. "But the Saxons never caught the gem bug. They make wine."

"Poor Megan is the younger sister to three brothers," Kimberley expanded. She nudged Ryan's arm. "It's bad enough having only one baby brother."

"Baby?" Ryan snorted and gave her a hard stare. "I'm taller than you, sister!"

Jessica flinched at the word *baby*. It must be worse for Kimberley, she decided. The renewed happiness between Kimberley and Ric had come at a price. Jessica had heard that Kimberley couldn't ever have children. It was so sad. So final. She touched her own stomach. She might not have Ryan's love, but she'd been fortunate enough to be blessed with a baby. She caught Ryan watching her.

Hurriedly Jessica produced the list of items she wanted to discuss and started to talk. The next half hour passed in a blur of discussion about security, models, stylists and jewellery while they ate. Only to be interrupted when Ryan's cell phone shrilled.

He picked it up and squinted at the number. "Caller ID blocked. I'm tempted not to answer it."

"Oh, go on, you know that you can't resist!" Kimberley scoffed. "And you'll only have to ring back later. Take the call, we'll forgive you. This time."

"Excuse me." Ryan rose to his feet and took the call a little way from their table. His answers were brief. Uncommunicative.

Jessica watched him out the corner of her eye as Kimberley checked through the points that had to be discussed at Monday's meeting.

"I'm not prepared to comment until we meet." Ryan's voice went up a notch. Kimberley's head shot up. Jessica watched him terminate the call with worried eyes.

"It never ends." Ryan sat down heavily. "That was one Tom Macnamara."

"If he's a journalist, you should've referred him to me, not agreed to meet him yourself," Kimberley rebuked her brother.

Ryan's mouth slanted. "He's not a journalist. He's a private investigator—from Macnamara Investigations."

Kimberley's breath caught in an audible gasp. "What does he want?"

Ryan's smile grew feral. "Money. What else?"

"Oh, no. Not another scandal." Kim paled at the prospect. "I don't know how much more we can take. What will it do to the share price—"

"Wait." Ryan held up a hand. "I should've clarified that he's not looking for a payoff. Nor is he threatening to go to the newspapers with whatever information he has. He wants payment of a bill that he says is due to him."

"What bill?" Kim asked. "And who retained him?"

Jessica's stomach cramped at the silence that followed. She glanced from Kimberley to Ryan's inscrutable face.

"It appears that our father did." Ryan directed the statement at Kim. "He claims that Dad hired him to find James—"

Kim waved a dismissive hand. "He's hardly the first."

"But he says that he's got a lead—" Ryan broke off as the waiter arrived with coffee. "He wants to meet with us. But first we have to pay him what he says he's due. Apparently the bill was sent to Ian Van Dyke, the lawyer killed in the crash."

"Oh," murmured Kimberley. "Of course, we'll pay him. But we want to hear what he has to say first."

"Exactly!" Ryan agreed. "I offered to meet him tomorrow. He says he's away, but he'll be back in Sydney in a couple of weeks. If he's a fraud, we'll expose him."

"But what if he's the real thing?" Kim whispered. "What if James is still alive?"

Jessica's eyes darted from one to the other.

Ryan's hand tightened around his coffee cup. Tension sizzled in the air.

"We'll deal with that when it happens." Ryan looked across at his sister.

"You should know that Ric told me this morning that there's a rumour that Matt Hammond caught a flight to Alice Springs."

"Hell." Ryan banged a fist on the table. "That's the last thing we need."

Jessica jumped. "What does that mean?" It was the first time she'd spoken. The other two turned to look at her, their expressions startled. She shrank back into her chair and resisted the urge to apologise. No, darn it. There was no need to apologise. Kimberley had invited her to talk about work, and Ryan had gate-crashed their meeting. She had every right to join in the conversation. She straightened her spine. She was every bit as good as a Blackstone.

"I'm sorry." Ryan thrust a hand through his hair, ruffling it. "I forgot that not everyone knows the dynamics of the rather complicated Blackstone family. Vincent lives in Coober Pedy, but he's in Alice Springs at present. If Matt's flown to Alice, it means he's after Vincent's shareholding."

"Oh." Jessica thought about that. "Would your Uncle Vincent sell?"

"That's the million-dollar question. Under normal circumstances, probably not." Ryan shrugged. "But opal prices have taken a hammering lately, and Vincent is no longer a young man. He may be ready to sell."

"The cousins won't let him sell," Kimberley said firmly.

"We can only hope that. But their main concern is their opal empire," Ryan responded.

"What happens if Matt gets those shares?" Jessica had a feeling that she wouldn't like the answer. She couldn't help thinking of Dani Hammond's fervent wish that the Hammond-Blackstone feud would end.

Kimberley leaned forward, a fine frown line marring her brow beneath a widow's peak. "Matt already has ten per cent he bought off Uncle William—"

Ryan muttered a less than complimentary assessment of dear Uncle William's parentage. Then added, "But with Vincent's shares, Matt would be looking dangerous. A couple more pockets of shares and he'd be in a very strong position to launch a hostile takeover of Blackstone's."

Jessica felt her mouth rounding into a startled *O*.

Ryan took another sip of coffee. "Some of my father's estate planning was less than perfect. The old bastard never thought he'd die so soon. He thought he had lots of time."

"Ryan!" Kim scolded.

Jessica looked from one to the other.

"It's the truth." Ryan spread his hands. "He thought he was immortal."

Like Ryan did.

It struck Jessica that Ryan had the same proud belief in his own infallibility that his father had held. Enough to verge on arrogance. Would Ryan follow in his father's footsteps?

"We need to make Vincent an offer. Beat Matt to it if we can."

"With Dad's personal fortune frozen until probate it will be difficult to stop Matt." Kimberley looked worried. "It will take a huge sum of money—more than we can spare right now—to buy more shares. We need to keep reserves on hand to run the business."

"You could raise a loan," Jessica suggested tentatively.

"Isn't that a contravention—"

"No." Ryan cut across Kim's protest. "Great idea, Jess." He gave her a smile of approval that made her shiver with delight. "But not from the company to buy its own shares. A loan from the bank—to one of us. Or several of us. We have enough assets in our own right to secure funds. I have shares and my penthouse, and there's the property you and Ric own."

Kim bit her lip. "I'll need to discuss it with Ric. The property is—"

Ryan didn't allow the protest to take hold. "We need to stop Matt before he destroys Blackstone's."

Jessica flinched at Ryan's steely tone. He sounded just like his father. A chip off the old block.

"We could also raise a loan against Miramare," Ryan said slowly.

"Miramare?" Kimberley's eyes widened.

"The first time I ever saw it was after the funeral. Before that I'd only ever seen photos of it," Jessica said.

"It's worth a millions," Kim said slowly.

"And as long as the executor of the estate is prepared to authorise the loan it shouldn't be too hard." Ryan put his coffee cup down and sat back. "Garth won't have a problem. With all our other combined assets, we shouldn't need to use the funds. We just want to make sure we have that extra line of credit available—in case we need it to fight Matt Hammond. I'll talk to the bank."

Kim looked anxious and although he patted her shoulder reassuringly, it was Jessica's gaze that Ryan sought.

"No photo could ever do Miramare justice," Ryan announced on Monday morning as the powerful BMW M6 braked in front of the glamorous triple-storey Italianate mansion. "Or Pemberley, as my mother apparently sometimes used to call this place. A joke, I think."

Jessica climbed out the car and looked around. Ryan had swept into the store an hour ago, after meeting with the event coordinator organising the jewellery show, and whisked her away to give her a tour of Miramare—all because of her casual comment at lunch last Friday that she'd never seen Miramare before the funeral.

He'd called over the weekend, told her he was at a loose end, and offered her a tour of Miramare, there and then.

Feeling besieged, she'd refused. He hadn't taken affront. Instead he'd invited her to come today while he met with the valuator. Compelled by curiosity for another glimpse at the house where he'd grown up, she'd accepted, deciding that it would be safe enough with a third person to keep them company.

Empty of the hordes that had been at the wake, the mansion looked so much bigger, so much grander than she remembered. It loomed over her and Ryan, emphasising the vast difference between her background and the manner in which Ryan had been raised.

A world apart.

Beyond the house lay a stunning view of the Sydney Harbour. Ryan headed for the front door and Jessica followed more slowly, her eyes scanning her surroundings, taking in the outbuildings with space to garage a dozen cars, the precisely clipped hedges that lined the street, the established trees and the manicured green lawns that spoke of the attention of full-time gardeners. Before Ryan could insert his key into the lock, the door swung open.

"About time you came to visit, Ryan."

Ryan shepherded Jessica through the door. "Jessica, meet Marcie, the most indispensable person in the entire household."

"Nice to meet you, Jessica. I'm the housekeeper," Marcie said in response to Jessica's smiled greeting. "Not his aunt, in case his introduction gave you that idea."

Bright white light spilled into the entrance hall from high-set windows. Jessica blinked. Then her eyes adjusted to the interior and she saw the double stairway with its intricate black wrought-iron balustrade that curved up to the next floor.

"Is Sonya at home?" Ryan asked from behind Jessica.

"She's meeting a friend this morning for tea," Marcie said, stopping and turning around.

"No worries, we're early for an appointment." Ryan grinned down at the older woman. "We don't need a hostess. But can I ask you to brew a pot of tea and bring it to the balcony?"

"I'll do better," Marcie replied with easy familiarity. "I'll bring out those freshly baked scones you love, too."

"Come," Ryan said, gesturing to Jessica. "I'll give you a quick tour of the house and then we'll go sit outside and have a cup of tea and a scone. The views are truly splendid from the balcony. We might as well take advantage of the sunshine while we wait for the valuator to arrive."

He led her from one room to another. Everything about Miramare was ornate and grand, beautiful to look at. But it was far removed from the comfortable, touchable kind of home Jessica's heart craved.

"Tea, I think," Ryan said at last and led her back to the living room.

As they stepped through the French doors, Jessica's breath caught at the view spread before them. "Gosh, you can even see the Sydney Harbour Bridge from here." The instantly recognisable arched structure dominated the skyline. "Who did you say inherits this place under the new will?"

"James, as the eldest son." Ryan's voice held a hint of self-mockery.

A rush of sympathy for Ryan engulfed her. Up until now she hadn't considered that Ryan and Kim might both lose the home where they had grown up. "But James is dead, so that makes you the eldest son. And Kim's left out completely?" She shook her head. "Your father never had much of an appreciation for women."

They headed over to a white wrought-iron table and chairs

perched near the edge of the balcony overlooking the swimming pool. Ryan pulled out a chair for Jessica. "My father was hard on both his offspring. But I might still inherit Miramare as the eldest son when James fails to show before August."

"But you're the one who's spent all these years working for your father." She sank down onto the chair and tilted her head to look at him, her hand shading her eyes from the sun.

Ryan dropped into the chair beside her and shrugged. "He never really forgave me for going off to South Africa after he brought Ric on board."

"He was too hard on his children. At least you won't repeat those mistakes with your own children." Jessica's lips curled into an ironic smile.

"Oh, no." He held up his hands as if warding off an attack. "I don't want children."

"I know—you told me. No cats. No kids. No press. No diamond rings."

"You remember."

Jessica couldn't decipher his expression. She decided it had to be relief. "How could I ever forget? But if you inherit Miramare," she said, the irony not lost on her, "then you'll have to rethink. You'll need a wife."

"Why would I need a wife?" Ryan shot her a look she couldn't read.

"Well, you'd have a mansion—not a jet-set penthouse— and you'd be in possession of a fortune. So you'd be in want of a wife."

He raised an eyebrow. "I'm not some Jane Austen hero."

And she was hardly Elizabeth Bennet. Jessica thought of what she'd overheard at the wake, when he'd said to Kimberley, not realising she'd come to offer comfort, *What makes you so certain that I'd want a wife like Jessica?* The words had sent her scuttling back across the room.

"No, you're not the marrying kind."

He looked startled for a moment. Then he said, "That was one thing about you, Jess, you always knew the score."

Ouch. "Yep, I knew the score. And after seeing this place, if I suspected it might be part of the marriage deal, it would most likely scare me away. So no pressure, Mr. Darcy!"

Ryan didn't laugh as she'd intended. After a moment's thought he said, "Not long ago I might've preferred that charlatan of an investigator to find James rather than to contemplate marriage."

It hurt that the idea of marrying her was so repugnant. Jessica looked away, determined not to let him see how much he'd gotten to her. Fortunately Marcie arrived with the tea and scones spread with butter and jam before the pause could become too pointed.

"Will you pour?" Ryan asked after Marcie had gone.

"Sure." Jessica filled two cups, topped them with milk and handed one cup to Ryan. He helped himself to a scone and took a bite. In the garden a gang of noisy sulphur-crested cockatoos landed in the trees on the boundary.

After a moment Jessica said, "I can imagine the pain that information from cranks and hoax calls must have brought your family."

"My father would run every lead down." Ryan brushed the crumbs off his fingers. "Even calls from fake psychics who claimed to have been in touch with James, to have talked to him and have messages from him for Mother. In every other aspect of his life he was totally in control—except when it came to James."

Howard's obsession must've been very hard for Kimberley and Ryan to live with. No wonder Ryan believed he'd never measured up to his dead brother. But she could also understand Howard's grief at losing a child. And, as the mother who had carried the baby in her body for nine months, Ursula must've been devastated, too. Jessica resisted the urge to touch her stomach, to stroke the swelling curve under her loose-fitting top. Just the thought of losing her unborn baby was enough to make her shudder.

She stared at the uneaten scone on her plate, then glanced back at Ryan. "It must've been terrible for your mother to be given fresh hope with each crank call and then be disappointed again."

"Mother wanted closure. She was responsible for commissioning a plaque in memory of James at Rookwood near where my grandfather is buried, but Howard would only let her put a date of birth on it. No date of death. In case James was still alive." The grooves beside Ryan's mouth deepened. "But at least Dad had a quest that kept him going. To build Blackstone's…and to find James. Mother had nothing—except her weekly Sunday afternoon visit to tend the rosebushes she'd planted around the plaque. In the end she gave up hope."

"She had two other children," Jessica pointed out softly, suddenly understanding why Blackstone's was so vitally important to Ryan. He didn't believe that James was alive, so he couldn't pursue that quest on his father's behalf. But he could continue to build Blackstone Diamonds. To make it richer, more powerful.

"She drowned herself, you know."

Before she could control it, Jessica's gaze flitted to the pool that lay blue and seemingly innocuous below the balcony.

"No, not here. At the beach house at Byron Bay."

"You were on *holiday* when your mother drowned herself?" What had made his mother do that?

Ryan nodded, his face closed. "A three-week getaway for Mother, Kimberley and me. Aunt Sonya was there, too—pregnant, I think, with Dani."

Picking up her teacup, Jessica took a sip. "Where was Howard?"

"Working."

Typical. She watched him over the edge of the teacup. "Oh."

Ryan must've caught the note of censure in her unguarded comment because he said quickly, a touch defensively, "He planned to arrive the day before Mother's birthday."

The information came in meagre drips, like water being extracted from a stone. Jessica felt guilty asking for more, but she'd never heard Ryan talk about his mother's death before. She doubted he ever had—even as a child. As he grew older she could imagine him trying not to do or say anything that his father might consider a sign of weakness. So he'd probably never discussed it at all. All that suppression could not have been healthy. She persisted. "Your mother drowned herself on her birthday?"

"No. Two weeks before. So Dad had to come early anyway."

There would've been no birthday party for his mother that year. Yet only a year earlier Ursula had celebrated her thirtieth birthday, here at Miramare. That night Ursula had fallen in the swimming pool in front of her guests—an uncanny portent of her suicide. And the night that had started as a birthday celebration had ended with the theft of the legendary Blackstone necklace.

"How…" Jessica's voice trailed away. She was going to ask how old had he been. Little more than a baby, she reasoned.

"How? Mother used to go for a swim alone in the sea each morning. One dawn she walked into the sea and never came back. At first we thought she'd gone for a swim and drowned by accident. But Aunt Sonya found the note. It was all hushed up. Dad liked to pretend that it was all a horrible mistake, an accident."

But the newspapers had not allowed Howard to continue

that fiction. Even now there was still wild speculation about Ursula Blackstone's death.

"No, no." Jessica was horrified that he might think she'd wanted all the gory details. "I was going to ask how old you were when it happened."

"I was three, so I don't remember it at all. It's more like a feeling of emptiness. And sometimes I smell things or hear a sound and get a flash of something I can barely remember."

In the tall trees a cockatoo screeched.

"How horribly sad."

"Kimberley was four when Mother died. She remembers more about Mother."

There was a touch of longing in Ryan's voice that caused Jessica's throat to close. She had a sudden picture of a lonely little boy standing at the front gate, waiting for his mother, or the memories of her to come back.

"Ryan." The housekeeper's call broke in. "Your visitors have just driven in. "I'll let them in and then I'm going to chase those cockatoos before they descend on the blueberry bushes."

"Visitors? I thought there was only a valuator?" Ryan rose to his feet. To Jessica he said, "Stay here, enjoy the sunshine. You haven't touched your scone. Marcie will scold you if you don't eat up. This shouldn't take long."

The hot sun was warm on her skin. Looking over the garden which Ryan would've played in as a child, Jessica shifted in her chair, uncomfortably conscious of his baby growing inside her body. Guilt niggled at her.

With each passing day, it became more pressing for her to tell him about the baby before he saw from the changes in her body. She'd delayed, frightened that he would demand that she get an abortion, but that deadline had now passed. It would no longer be safe.

But the thought of telling him, of losing the amiability that had been growing between them, distressed her.

By the time Ryan returned, Jessica was feeling drowsy from the hot sun. The cockatoos had vanished at the sight of Marcie brandishing a broom, and she'd eaten not one but two of the delicious scones and was dreading the thought of climbing onto the scale tomorrow morning. Right now her weight was rocketing up like the mercury on a sweltering day. If she didn't stop eating so much, she was going to look like a whale by the time she started to show.

"That's taken care of. The valuator brought a banker along who thinks the bank may not grant the loan unless James comes to life and consents to the application." Ryan frowned a little. "Or we wait until August when that provision expires."

"How crucial is it to get the loan in place?" Jessica asked.

"Ric and I are simply being cautious in case we need funds available to fight Matt on a takeover bid. And there's still the security of the Byron Bay property, as well as my penthouse and Ric and Kim's new home."

"Surely you won't need to be present for those valuations, will you?"

"Not really—certainly not for the valuation of Ric and Kim's home. But I'd like to make sure that the valuator gives each property the most favourable value. My presence will do that."

Ryan was definitely a control freak. But he was probably right. His presence would make a difference. Yet Jessica couldn't help thinking of Ryan returning to the house in Byron Bay that must hold painful memories of his mother.

"When will you go up to Byron Bay?"

"Wednesday, I think. My diary can be cleared. I'll probably fly up and back in the same day."

He'd be all alone. Jessica's heart melted at the thought of him confronting the ghostly memories that must lurk in the beach house. It would be the first time that he had visited since his father died. And she couldn't help thinking that seeing the beach house might give her some insight into the man who'd been her lover…the man who would be the father of her child.

Jessica rapidly considered her own schedule. "I've got a lot of leave due to me. I could take a day off—if my boss approves." She hesitated. "Would you like me to come and keep you company?"

The look Ryan gave her was impenetrable. "I would. And don't worry about taking leave. You work hard enough as it is. I have an early appointment with the security contractors for the show, so I'll be in the store a little later than normal. I'll pick you up midmorning."

Eight

Jessica was keeping an eye open for Ryan on Wednesday morning when Kimberley Perrini twirled into the showroom and did a little dance around the floor. "Jarrod Hammond is coming."

The show to unveil the new collections was now less than ten days away. Instantly Jessica got the significance of Matt Hammond's brother's attendance—and Kim's exhilaration. "Does this mean Matt is coming, too?" More importantly did it herald the beginning of the end of the Blackstone-Hammond feud?

Kimberley stopped dancing and flung her hands out wide. "Who knows? He certainly hasn't replied to the invitation I asked Holly to send him. And he's not talking to me."

"So probably not."

Kimberley's eyes darkened. "I don't like being at odds with Matt. As well as being great to work for, he was a great friend."

"Then I need tips from you," Jessica said cryptically.

"On what? How to keep your boss as a friend? I don't think I've done too well in that department." Kimberley put a slim hand on Jessica's arm, her diamond engagement ring scintillating in the light. "My brother is a tough guy, a man of few words, but I'm certain you mean a lot to him."

Jessica sighed. "Not nearly enough."

"Jessica." Kimberley leaned forward. "I know my brother can be—" she paused, searching for the right word "—uncommunicative. But he's been through plenty in the last two months. Dad's disappearance. The recovery of his body. Then he had to identify Dad's remains. That must have been hell. And he's recently buried those remains. On the same day that it became public knowledge that Dad had left a fortune to Marise, a very stunning, much younger woman. And her son is now pretty much set up for life, too. God knows what Ryan thought of that! And that's before you remember that Uncle William's selling his shares to Matt…and Matt's threat to go all out for revenge is making it incredibly tough on the work front. It's been truly awful. I know how much it's affected me—and I'm not as self-contained as Ryan. Give him time."

Put like that, his problems made her own seem suddenly trivial. But then Jessica thought of the baby. Of the days—weeks—ticking by. Her body was swelling, growing ripe. Any day now she'd start to show. The flowing dressy tops she'd been wearing lately teamed with black trousers would soon attract comment. "Time is the one luxury I don't have."

But Kimberley's words stayed with her and when Ryan arrived to pick her up for their day trip to Byron Bay, she found herself searching his face for signs of strain. And forgiving him when he seemed a little distracted.

A car was waiting for them at the airport, and the drive to the town centre took less than thirty minutes.

The beach house turned out to be a historic five-bedroom

house sited a little below Australia's most easterly lighthouse on Wategos Beach. The boundary on the street frontage was edged with Norfolk pines and when the car turned into the drive, Jessica caught her breath at the immaculately maintained tropical garden dominated by palms and lush plantings. *Beach house* was definitely a misnomer.

"It's beautiful."

"I've come here often over the years," Ryan said. "My father used to spend most of his time away from work here. It was the only time he and I ever had alone. Kimberley never visits—the memories are too bad. She doesn't even swim." A glimpse of pain flared in Ryan's eyes, then it was gone. "Come, let's go in. The valuator should be here by now."

The valuator was already skirting the outside taking notes. Jessica went into the house that Ryan had unlocked to give Ryan the opportunity to talk freely. From the large wooden windows she could see that the house had been positioned to maximise the impact of the view from inside the house. The living room faced over rolling green lawns to a wide vista of blue sea. She didn't know how long she stood there, just soaking in the beauty.

"There are quite a few pods of dolphins who make Byron Bay their home." Ryan had come up soundlessly behind her. Jessica struggled to keep her composure as his warm breath winnowed her hair as he spoke. "And in winter the humpback whales come to visit. The bay is full of stingrays." His arms slid around her from behind, and his chin rested on her shoulder, his cheek against her hair.

Jessica heard a car starting as the valuator departed. "Your holidays were very different from mine, although we also went to the beach. When I was growing up, we used to go camping every Christmas. And when I was about seven my parents bought a battered secondhand caravan that they towed down to Lakes Entrance and left there during the year. My father was a mechanic so he was good at fixing things up. Every holiday we'd go down there, just the three of us." She leaned back in the circle of his arms, breathed in his warm manly scent and looked up at him with a nostalgic smile. "That was our beach house. Yet that's where I spent some of the happiest times of my life."

"What happened to change that?"

"When I was ten years old my father had an accident at work." Jessica looked down, veiling her eyes.

"At the funeral I couldn't help wondering why he was in a wheelchair. But I didn't want to pry. You must get sick of endless questions."

"I don't mind. I'm so proud of my father." She paused, then added, "Ironically enough, after his accident things got a little easier financially and we used to hire a holiday apartment after that, one with ramps for wheelchairs." She tried not to stiffen in his arms, not to withdraw.

"At least your parents had insurance."

Jessica didn't contradict him. It was better for Ryan to believe that. She freed herself from his arms and took a step away. "And I went to boarding school. I got awfully homesick. I missed home, my mum and my dad."

"Which one did they send you to?"

"Pymble Ladies' College."

Ryan looked startled. "That's where Kimberley went to school."

"I know." Jessica knew he must be wondering how a mechanic could justify such expensive school fees—even with an insurance payout. "She was a senior when I arrived. I was very much in awe of her especially when she became head girl."

"It's not something I often admit out aloud, but my sister

is a very special person." He gave her a conspiratorial grin. But then his eyes became serious. "What did we talk about for the last two years? How much more is there that I don't know about you? I don't think it's only me who talks too little. It wasn't only me avoiding intimacy in our relationship, was it, Jess?" He raised an eyebrow.

It was true. They'd both avoided intimacy, Jessica thought. It had been convenient to tell herself that all the faults lay on his side—his lack of commitment, his ruthless inflexibility, his Blackstone pride.

But she'd been so careful to hide so much of herself, too. If she wanted this burgeoning relationship between them to continue, she was going to have to open herself up to him. As difficult as that might be.

At last the lack of communication between them was emerging, the hurts, the disappointments, the unspoken dreams. And it gave her hope, hope that they could both change the parts of themselves that had blocked their chances at happiness before.

When he suggested that they go for a drive to see the lighthouse, Jessica jumped at it. They were too alone here in this place. Too secluded. And she had some thinking to do before she shared all the secrets.

An hour later after a climb to the top of the headland where the lighthouse was located, they made their way back down again and Ryan produced a picnic hamper.

"You think of everything," Jessica sighed in bliss as she drew out a bottle of Bundaberg ginger beer. From where they sat on the sunlit grass below the lighthouse, the bay stretched out in front of them. And, except for the shrill calls of the silver gulls and the whisper of the sea wind, there was absolute silence.

After they'd eaten the dainty smoked salmon sandwiches,

and snacked on biscuits with wedges of camembert, Jessica asked, "What will happen to the beach house now that your father is gone?"

Ryan lay on his back with his arms folded behind his head. "In terms of the will it comes to me. I'll sell it as soon as I can."

"Oh."

He turned his head. "You wouldn't sell it in my place?"

"I don't know. I can understand the terrible memories it brings. But it was also a place where your mum spent time with you and your sister. Where you spent time with your father. Maybe you should wait before you rush to sell."

There was a moment's charged silence. Then he said, "Maybe I will. Unless we need to raise funds in a hurry to fend off Matt."

Matt Hammond again. Jessica looked down at the face she'd grown to love so much and wished that he was less like his father. "Don't you think that the Blackstones and the Hammonds should try and end this feud before it causes more unhappiness?"

"I'd be happy to end it."

Jessica felt a surge of relief. Perhaps Ryan was different from his father after all.

"But only if Matt Hammond backs off from buying our stock—and his father apologises for stealing the Blackstone Rose. Matt Hammond needs to make the first move."

Or perhaps, Jessica thought, not so much had changed at all.

Matt Hammond needs to make the first move.
The words stayed with Jessica, keeping her awake deep into the night. So the following morning, as soon as she reached her office in the Blackstone's store, Jessica picked up the telephone before she could chicken out. Ryan *would*

appreciate what she was about to do, Jessica assured herself, her heart knocking against her ribs, as she dialled the number. "Matt Hammond, please."

If only Matt would come to the launch, that might be the first conciliatory step toward bridging the feud. And maybe then Ryan would not be quite so intransigent in his demands of what was required to end this ridiculous feud—especially if Kim could convince him.

Jessica almost fainted with relief on being told that Matt was in a meeting.

Struggling for composure, she left a message asking him to call her back. After she set the handset down she started to shake. What on earth was she thinking? Ryan would not welcome her interference.

But then she picked up the brochure for the launch that lay on the counter and started leafing through the pages. She saw the work of all the talented designers that Blackstone's used, and of the new designers, like Dani Hammond, who were being groomed to become big names.

She thought about the lustrous pearls that Matt was famed for sourcing. A vision that had started out as insignificant as a grain of sand in an oyster grew clearer in her mind. The excitement that churned in her stomach whenever she had an idea that the market later caught on to told her that it would work. And Xander Safin would be the perfect person to bring the vision to crafted life.

The morning passed in a rush. Jessica was talking to her mother on the phone, arranging to have dinner with her parents, when Ryan walked into her office and turned the chair in front of her desk around before straddling it. Folding his arms across the top, he rested his chin on it and smiled at her.

It was a smile full of charm and affection. It did strange

things to her and caused her heartbeat to speed up. Jessica cut short her conversation with her mother. But before she could greet him the ringing phone cut in, stalling a reply. She signalled for him to stay.

This was the relaxed version of Ryan she'd fallen in love with in Adelaide. But in the time she'd lived with him she'd discovered there was so much more depth and character under the superficial charm and wonderful manners that always made her feel like a woman in a million.

"Ms Cotter?" The voice was deep, with a hint of Trans-Tasman accent.

Her breath caught. "Jessica, please. May I call you back a little later?" She sent Ryan a guarded glance. He slanted her a wicked smile.

"I'm afraid I'll be out for the rest of the day and tomorrow. So it will be a couple of days before you will reach me."

Jessica fought an unfamiliar urge to swear. Of all the hours in the day why did Matt Hammond have to call now?

Drawing a deep breath, she launched into speech. "I've a proposition to put to you. I've heard you source amazing pearls."

"I like to think so." There was a hint of humour in Matt's voice and Jessica relaxed a little. Maybe this would not be as difficult as she had anticipated.

"I'd like to be frank with you. I've been struggling to find the kind of pearls Blackstone's need."

Over the line she could feel the sudden chill at the introduction of the Blackstone name. Jessica told herself she was being oversensitive. She rushed on. "I'd like to use House of Hammond pearls in a range of jewellery designed by Xander Safin to be available for next year's northern summer."

"I take it these designs will be carried by Blackstone's stores?"

"Yes, as part of a new collection to be launched next year—a whole new take on the Sea Meets Sky collection Xander Safin has crafted."

"Is the board aware of your proposition, Ms Cotter?"

Across the desk her gaze tangled with Ryan's. He was shaking his head and motioning that he wanted her to end the conversation. Without a doubt, Ryan knew who was on the other end of the line. "No."

"Perhaps you should discuss this with the directors first. You may find that what you propose is not welcome."

Jessica looked away from Ryan's irate face and chewed at the inside of her cheeks. "I needed to know that you would be willing to supply Blackstone's first. I was hoping that we could discuss this further at the launch."

Jessica's pulse was racing. She'd come this far, she wasn't backing off now. She thought about Kim. About how Matt Hammond's remoteness was hurting her. She thought about Ryan. About the feud and its effect on him.

"You will be coming, won't you?"

Ryan was saying something to her now, his voice fierce. She blocked it out.

"No, I won't be attending," Matt Hammond said with a finality that indicated that the conversation was over.

Jessica rushed on. "But your brother is coming."

She sneaked a glace at Ryan. His face was even blacker than before. Jessica forced herself not to let his displeasure sway her. She told herself that it was for his own good. She tried to convince herself that he would one day thank her. She nearly succeeded—until she heard the sputtering sound coming from his direction.

"Jarrod?" For the first time she caught a hint of uncertainty in Matt's voice. Apparently he hadn't known that. "Jarrod will be there?"

"Yes, he contacted Kim for an invitation." Jessica didn't dare look at Ryan.

A moment later Matt responded. No chinks in that hard voice remained. "That's his concern. And, Ms. Cotter?"

"Yes?" Jessica had a feeling she wouldn't like what was coming next.

"It won't be long before all the pearls in Blackstone pieces will come from the House of Hammond."

It was a threat. A threat of a man who had vowed to take over the empire Howard Blackstone had built. Was Ryan correct? Did Matt want to destroy everything that the Blackstones had built?

When Jessica set down the handset she discovered that her hands were shaking. She couldn't decide which of the two men was harder or more proud.

"That was Matt Hammond, wasn't it? Did you call him first?"

Jessica gave a start. Ryan stood beside her, his mouth drawn tight, his shoulders tense. Despite his deceptively mild tone, Jessica realized he was seething with rage.

"Does it matter? He won't supply the pearls I need for next season's designs, nor is he coming to the launch."

Softly, dangerously, Ryan said between his teeth, "If I hadn't been sitting here when the call came in, you would never have told me that you'd contacted him."

"What was the point? He refused." Jessica felt overwhelmed by a deflating sense of failure.

"You would have lied to me by omission."

Jessica's gaze leaped to his.

"Like you lied before," he continued.

Her heart started to pound with apprehension. "When?"

"You never told me you were going to Auckland in my father's jet."

That again. "I missed my plane to Auckland. I didn't see

any need to let you know. You and I weren't talking, remember?" The memory of the argument they'd had seemed like a lifetime ago.

Desperate for a sign that she wasn't wasting her time in a dead-end relationship, Jessica had pushed for an invitation to spend Christmas and New Year with him. It would've been their second Christmas together and she'd wanted more than separate vacations. As little as Jessica wanted to spend vacation time with Howard Blackstone at Byron Bay, she'd needed Ryan to prove his commitment to her by spending Christmas together, to be reassured that she'd be more than his secret mistress for the coming year.

But Ryan had made it icily clear that Christmas at Byron Bay was off-limits. She'd been wounded and she'd lashed out. They'd fought and parted in anger. Then two days before New Year's Day Jessica had discovered she was pregnant— and her whole life had swung upside down. It had been the final nail in the coffin of their precarious affair.

"I don't like you keeping secrets, Jessica."

The baby. Her gaze slid away from his. Guilt surged in her chest, along with a tight, uncomfortable feeling of regret.

He'd had his chance.

"Look at me." She met the dark jade eyes, heard the ragged breath he drew. "I want to start over…with everything out in the open."

"Make me your public mistress?" She heard the distaste in her voice and knew he must have, too. "I don't think so, Ryan."

Slowly he came towards her. She had lots of time to turn her head away, but she didn't. Instead she held his gaze.

When his lips took hers, she let herself open up like the petals of a flower unfurling to the sun, kissing him back with all the emotion and intensity she could dredge up, trying to communicate her feelings about him.

He drew back, confusion written all over his handsome features. "You respond to me like that? But you refuse to be my lover. What do you want?"

She bit her lip. "A couple of months ago a little commitment would've been good. But now I'm not sure if that's what you really want or if you're only making the noises you think I want to hear."

"I want to make our relationship public."

"Because the biggest critic is dead?"

"This is not about my father." Now there was annoyance in his tone; the softness had vanished. "Everyone knows I'm against workplace relationships."

Making their relationship public would be a huge concession for him, Jessica realised. But she wanted more. She would no longer be satisfied with anything less than his love.

Slowly she shook her head. "I'm sorry, Ryan, it's no longer enough."

"Is this about marriage? Because I don't want—"

"Relax, this isn't about marriage. It's about me. About what I want. And I don't want to be your lover, nor do I want to marry you." At least, not while things stood so badly between them. Not while he didn't love her. And certainly not while she was lying to him.

Ryan was right, she was keeping secrets. Well, no more. She drew a deep breath. "I'm pregnant, Ryan."

Whatever he'd been about to say escaped in a whoosh of air. He stared at her, clearly stunned.

"And, before you ask, yes, it is your baby."

"I wasn't going to dispute that." A frown gouged deep lines between his eyes. "When did you find—"

"And, no, I won't be working after the baby is born—"

"Nor did I ask that," he interrupted, the lines of irritation marring his features.

"At least not for a while," Jessica continued as if he hadn' spoken. "I'll get through the launch and then I'll work my notice. You'll need to find someone else to run the Sydney store. I'm resigning."

"You can't leave!" He looked poleaxed. "You love the store."

"The baby will come first. I can't do justice to a high-flyer job and be a single parent. I want to spend time with my baby." A softening filled her as she spoke the words and she realised that was what she truly wanted. To spend time with the baby she and Ryan had created. She had no future with a man who was following in the footsteps of a man she despised. And she had no intention of spending her life with a man who was never at home.

"You've thought it all through," he said slowly. "You've got it all planned." He didn't look thrilled at the prospect Jessica could see the wheels turning in his mind. "What about me? Where's my place in all this?"

The first twinge of uncertainty pierced her. He'd never wanted children, so why did he look so unhappy? "You'll always be my baby's father, Ryan. You're welcome to visit whenever you want." She'd made her choice. And Ryan's life his priorities, were too different from hers. Jessica doubted she'd see much of him after the baby was born. But she knew he'd get a team of lawyers onto it, that his rights would be spelled out, that the baby would be given all the financial support he or she would ever need. "And don't worry that I'll be looking for support for myself. I've always been a careful saver and I've a healthy nest egg built up which will allow me time before I need to go back to work."

"Of course I'll contribute." His teeth snapped shut. "What if I want joint custody?"

Jessica laughed. She couldn't help herself. "Oh, Ryan There's no space in your executive bachelor lifestyle for a cat

Where would you fit a baby?" *No cats. No kids. No press. No diamond rings.* She knew his creed by rote.

He swallowed, slid off the chair and headed for the door, his haste revealing his desperation to escape. "This is a huge shock. I need to think about it."

"Don't worry about it." She watched him freeze in the doorway, his shoulders hunched. "You have enough on your mind with Matt's takeover bid."

In the course of the morning, despite being incredibly busy, Jessica found herself mulling over Ryan's unexpected reaction to the announcement of her pregnancy.

She'd expected him to feel trapped. He'd never wanted a family. Already he was trapped in the obligations to his family, to the company. She had expected him to be shocked. What she hadn't expected was his apparent desire to be involved in the baby's life beyond superficial financial support—his remark about joint custody had shocked her to the core.

But with the launch getting closer by the day, Jessica barely had time to breathe, much less think about custody arrangements as she fielded calls from Kimberley, as well as Holly and a host of caterers and security contractors and designers to finalise the finer details.

A couple of hours later, with Kimberley in a meeting and not taking calls, Jessica found herself on the phone to Ryan, stiltedly arranging to pay a quick visit to Miramare to make the final selection of paintings from Howard's collection. The paintings would be hung downstairs in the gallery-style lobby for the launch.

"I'll meet you at Miramare in an hour," Ryan stated, without mentioning the baby bombshell she'd dropped earlier.

"No, no." The last thing she wanted was to see him again

today. She needed time to think his reaction through. "Just let Marcie know I'm coming."

"I'll be there."

And the line went dead.

Jessica was apprehensive when she parked her Toyota in front of the mansion for the second time that week. To top it all, she was hot, irritated and totally out of sorts.

And of course, Ryan looked gorgeous, groomed and totally together, not a hair out of place, no sign of sweat from the sweltering Sydney heat.

Keeping her spine stiff to conceal that the heat was causing her to wilt, she strode beside him through the downstairs reception rooms, once again struck by the opulence, the grandeur. In the grand salon she picked out two modern paintings that would fit in with the mood of the launch. Ryan promised to have them sent over. The insurance for the transfer was already in place.

In the air-conditioned living room a large family oil portrait dominated one wall. Jessica stopped to admire it. A young and very beautiful Ursula, dressed in flowing white, knelt on a carpet of grass studded with white daisies under the wide branches of an oak tree. Beside her stood a small boy—James?—clutching a teddy bear and a baby clad in a pale pink dress in a bassinet. Howard stood behind the family, while, in the background, horses grazed on the hillside.

It was a picture of wealthy pastoral bliss. Jessica searched the painting. "You're not there."

Ryan barely spared the painting a glance. "I wasn't born yet. Mother was pregnant with me at the time." For a moment she thought he was going to add something about her own pregnancy, then to her intense relief, he said, "Look, why don't you use this picture over on this wall in the show?"

"I'll look now." But Jessica didn't move. Her attention

was fixed on Ursula Blackstone. Now she noticed the rounded belly that the dress's fullness concealed so cleverly. "Your mother looks so happy."

"That was painted before James…disappeared. After that she became very depressed, and when I was born, the depression worsened."

"Some women do feel blue after the birth." Jessica had been reading about the baby blues. In fact, she'd been reading everything she could lay her hands on to do with pregnancy and birth. Jessica-the-mother-to-be would bore Ryan to tears.

"Her depression pushed my father away. But he stood by her. It was only after her death that he started to have affairs."

She could see that the admission cost him. "Your father never brought his mistresses here, did he?"

"What?"

"Your father kept his affairs at work, separate from his family."

"If you mean that he had affairs with secretaries then yes, he kept his affairs at work." He glanced at her. "Although Marise wasn't strictly a secretary—"

"This isn't about Marise. It's about you. Until the funeral I'd never seen Miramare, much less set foot inside. You were following the patterns of behaviour your father had set. You would never have brought me here while I was your lover."

"Jess—"

"You didn't want your mistress to cross the threshold."

"You're wrong about that! It wasn't because you were my lover that I didn't want our relationship made public." He pushed a hand through his hair in a harassed manner. "It was because I didn't want to follow in my father's footsteps, sleeping with the staff. I've always been appalled by that."

"Sleeping with the staff?" she repeated.

"God, that sounds awful. Makes me sound like a total

snob. And that's not the reason why I'm against work relationships. They're disruptive, bad for the company."

"So why did you ever have an affair with me?"

"Because—" He stopped and shook his head. "It's too
hard to explain. I'm not sure I know the answer myself.
Except that I didn't seem capable of resisting you."

So he thought her irresistible. What did that mean? "But
you have very firm ideas about what kind of woman you
would not marry. A woman like me. I heard you at the wake
telling your sister you wouldn't marry a woman like me."

He caught her hands. "Jessica, I've been an arrogant jerk.
Your value is beyond—"

"My value as a staff member to Blackstone's?"

He paused. "Yes." Then he saw her face. "But that's not
all. You mean a lot to me as…" His voice trailed away.

"As a lover?"

"Yes!" He looked relieved.

"But never as a wife."

He didn't answer, and his eyes held shadows that made it
impossible to fathom what he was thinking. With a sigh,
Jessica turned on her heel and walked away to the French
doors. She stared out absently, noting how the sky reflected in
the sea, making the harbour appear even bluer than usual.
"You know, when I stayed with Mother over the Christmas
holidays, I told her there was someone I was seeing. She's
wanted me to get married for a long time. Finally, on New
Year's Day, I told her it was you." Her mother had been con-
flicted—partly thrilled, partly fearful that Jessica would be
hurt.

"So you wanted me to propose for your mother's sake?"

Jessica wished she'd never started this conversation. She
pushed the door open. Ryan followed, his hands shoved deep
into the pockets of his trousers. Before she knew it, she was

standing beside the broad expanse of the swimming pool. "My mother said a Blackstone would never marry someone like me." And she'd been right.

"What made your mother think she knew how I would react?" He pulled his hand out of his pocket. In the palm lay a ring box covered in midnight blue velvet. "Jessica—"

"Don't!" Jessica shut her eyes in horror. How had this happened? She didn't want his proposal now. It was much too late. She'd never be sure why he married her. Heck, it couldn't be for love.

"Why not?"

He was only asking her to marry him out of some chivalrous impulse because of the baby. "I can't. My mother is right. You…me…it wouldn't work."

"Now who's the snob?"

She shook her head frantically. *"I can't.* I don't want to be married to a carbon copy of Howard Blackstone. I want a husband, a family—not a megalomaniac intent on building an empire without thought of the cost to his humanity."

He stepped closer. She fended him off. He came closer still. Desperately Jessica gave him a push to hold him at bay. She couldn't cope with his kisses. Not now. Her eyes widened as he reeled backward. "Look out!"

Ryan hit the water with a splash, his arms flailing as he tried in vain to keep his balance. When he rose, his hair was plastered against his head, the water streaming off the shoulders of his suit jacket. He pulled it off and hoisted himself onto the side of the pool. His shirt clung to muscles she knew were every bit as hard as they looked. In one movement he unbuttoned the top buttons and yanked the shirt over his head.

Jessica made a strangled noise in her throat and gave his naked torso a furtive once-over. *Goodness, but he was beautiful.* "Have you still got the ring?"

"You want to reconsider?"

"No, but I'd hate for you to lose it." That sounded flippant. Jessica tore her eyes away from the glorious view of skin and muscle before she said something even more stupid.

He shifted, and, unable to resist, she took another peek. He was dabbing the wet shirt at the rivulets of water on his chest, trying to mop up the excess. She suppressed an offer to help.

"You haven't even seen what I was going to offer you."

"I can't accept it." She turned away from his sheer overwhelming masculinity. She needed to get out of here before she was tempted to give in to a bunch of crazy impulses. To touch him. To marry him. To do whatever he asked, even though she knew it wasn't what he'd planned for his life.

He'd be marrying her for all the wrong reasons.

"Dinner was scrummy tonight, thanks, Mum."

Sally Cotter turned from where she was packing the dirty dinner dishes into the dishwasher and smiled with pleasure. "Scrummy? It's years since I've heard you use that word."

Jessica had craved the familiarity of her parent's company tonight, and comfort food was precisely what she'd needed.

"Where can I put these?" The empty lasagne dish balanced precariously on top of the plate she held.

"Give it to me, love."

"Mum…" Jessica paused. "I wanted to tell you Ryan asked me to marry him today."

Her mother straightened. "Oh, Jessica! That's wond—"

"I turned him down." Jessica didn't want her mother getting her hopes up.

"You turned him down? But why?" Confusion churned in her mother's eyes. "It's your dream come true."

"No, Mother. It's *your* dream come true."

Her mother gave a start of surprise.

Jessica sighed. "I only wanted Ryan's love. I wanted him to be proud to proclaim it to the world, not keep me hidden away like some sordid secret. Without his love, a diamond ring—even the finest Blackstone fancy pink—is worthless."

Dishtowel in hand, Sally stood staring at Jessica. "But you love him. You admitted that on New Year's Day."

"If you remember, I also said it was all one-sided—all on my side—and that I was going to go back and break it off."

"But you didn't. So I thought—"

"Because only a few hours later, Ryan's father's plane went missing."

Sally tossed the dishtowel down and came toward her. "Maybe your love will be enough—"

"No, Mum. It can never be enough. You should know that." Her mother paled, her lips whiter than the tall lilies in the vase on the table. Instantly Jessica felt dreadful. She reached out and touched her mother's arm. "I'm sorry. I shouldn't have said that."

"Shouldn't have said what?" The whirr of wheels heralded Peter Cotter's arrival.

"Hello, Dad." Jessica withdrew her hand.

"I'll get us all a cup of tea." Her mother rushed into the pantry.

Jessica forced a stiff smile. "Do you want some French vanilla ice cream?"

"Maybe later." Peter Cotter's gaze was watchful. "You're not giving your mother a hard time are you, Jess?"

Jessica drew a deep breath. "I came to tell her that Ryan Blackstone asked me to marry him and I refused."

"Probably for the best."

"You're right." So why did it ache so much? "But Daddy, I wish I had said yes."

"Come here." Her father opened his arms and Jessica flew to

him. She hugged him awkwardly, the armrest of the wheelchair digging into her side. He smelt of the aftershave her mother bought him every Christmas and faintly of cigarette smoke.

"You've been smoking."

"Hush, don't tell your mother."

Jessica wagged her finger at him. "Daddy, you shouldn't be keeping secrets."

All humour disappeared when she read the knowledge that lay in her father's gaze. "Good advice, Jessica. So when are you intending to tell us about the baby?"

"Baby?" She could feel the blood draining from her face.

"Yes. Your and Ryan Blackstone's baby."

"How did you know?"

"A little observation. You were ill at the funeral. You've been complaining of nausea. You're not drinking coffee. Your mother was the same when she was pregnant with you."

The sound of china shattering caused them both to look up.

"You're pregnant?" Shock silvered her mother's eyes. "Is your father right? Is it Ryan's baby?"

Jessica nodded.

"Have you told Ryan?" her mother was asking.

"Yes."

"Is that why he asked you to marry him?"

Jessica hesitated. "Maybe. I think so. I don't know. Oh, Mum, my head is a mess!"

"I should've known a Blackstone would never bring you anything but pain."

"I've already broken it off."

Her mother slumped down onto a kitchen chair. "You need to leave Blackstone's."

"I've resigned. But I'm going to miss Blackstone's." And Ryan. Unbearably.

Her mother had struck the heart of her dilemma. She loved

working at Blackstone's—and hated the idea of leaving. An image of Kimberley Perrini flashed into her mind. Kim had left Blackstone's and gone to work for House of Hammond but it had been a time of drought for her. And Jessica knew she would feel a similar sense of loss.

But she had no choice.

She wanted a clean break. From Ryan. From Blackstone's. She stepped away from her father's wheelchair. She would see the show through. When the baby was older she would start looking for another job. She'd told Howard Blackstone that she'd quit after their terrible confrontation, only hours before his jet disappeared.

She should've cut her losses then, walked away and never come back. As much as she loved Ryan Blackstone, their relationship could never have a happy ending.

Later, as her mother came to see her off, Sally said, "Your father has forgiven me, Jessica. Why can't you?"

Jessica halted just short of the garden gate, and before she could stop herself, the words escaped. "How could have you let Howard Blackstone seduce you?"

Her mother's hand dropped away from the latch and the gate clicked shut again. "It's so hard to explain. Howard was so compelling. Attractive, successful, wealthy. A widower. He appreciated me." Sally drew a shuddering breath. "It started off as a light flirtation—"

Jessica raised an eyebrow. "With your boss?"

"I was a temp—everything was so tough back then. Before I knew it, I was in his bed." Sadness clouded her mother's eyes. "Your father was in a bad way after the accident. You were only ten when it happened—when that car fell off the jack on top of him mangling his legs. Things were hard. Without my job, without Howard Blackstone, everything would have been a lot worse. Howard was my escape. He gave me a job, took me to places I'd never seen, bought me clothes I could not afford. He gave me a glimpse of another world and made me feel like a princess."

"But you were married, Mum."

"I know." Her mother sucked in her cheeks and leaned against the gate. "And I hurt your father. But even worse, you found out and you disapproved. Your disapproval made me feel so guilty, I was almost relieved when Howard arranged for you to go board at Pymble Ladies' College, and offered to pay for you. Your father and I would never have been able to give you such a wonderful education."

Jessica had always suspected Howard had wanted her out of the way while he conducted a raging affair with her mother. He had disliked her intensely and had hated it when her mother had taken her along to meet him at out-of-the way cafes on those Friday afternoons. Of course, her mother had sworn her to silence about those trysts, and she'd felt like a silent accomplice.

Worst of all, as a teenager Jessica had read Howard's notes and letters to her mother. She'd found the box where her mother had hidden them on the top shelf of her closet and read them all. Some of them were seductive. Some were romantic. And some were downright frightening. Like the note that must've been sent after a pregnancy scare where Howard had made it clear that if Sally ever fell pregnant, she would have to get an abortion.

"Will you ever forgive me?" Her mother's eyes were bleak and troubled.

Jessica blinked back the moisture in her eyes. "Oh, Mum, I *do* forgive you. Maybe because I understand more than you think. I've made the same mistake. I've fallen in love with my boss. But I've been even more stupid than you ever were. I fell pregnant."

"At least you're not married to another man—a man who is injured and needs you—nor do you have a young daughter at home waiting for you to come home while you attend illicit meetings with your lover." Her mother's eyes were full of self-loathing. "And at least Ryan Blackstone has offered to marry you."

"Oh, Mum." Jessica stared blindly over Sally's shoulder to where a car droned past on the suburban road. She remembered how frigid she'd been when years ago she'd discovered what those out-of-the-way encounters meant. That her mother was Howard Blackstone's lover. How she'd hated discovering halfway through her schooling where the money for her fancy girls' school funding came from.

Despite her reluctance to maintain any ties with Howard, she'd taken the job he had arranged for her when she turned seventeen only because it offered an escape to Melbourne. She'd been relieved to escape the strange relationship her parents shared, to gain financial independence. Ironically, driving her away had brought Sally to her senses and caused her mother to break off her relationship with Howard and leave his employ. But Jessica had already been gone; she hadn't been there to help her mother pick up the pieces and put her life back together again.

She put a hand over her mother's where it rested on her arm and clasped it tightly. "I was a right royal brat, wasn't I?"

"You had every right to be. I should never have had an affair. I put you into an impossible position. You were very loyal to your father."

"It must've been hard for you."

"It was. But Howard gave me an escape, some time away from home, where I could pretend your father's accident never happened."

"Oh, Mum. I love you."

Sally's smile was bittersweet. "The Blackstones are fabulously wealthy. Ryan was always a very nice youth. Polite. But all I want for you is to find someone to love you."

Jessica threw her arms around her mother. "With you and Dad to love me—and the baby—why do I need a husband?"

Nine

After the upheavals of the week, Jessica slept most of the weekend away. There was no doubt that her body was changing, swelling, growing fuller each passing day. Driving to work on Monday morning she told herself that once the launch was past, she would make up for all the stress by sleeping for a week.

Her work day did not start well. She walked into the showroom to be met with the news that Emma, one of the salesladies, had called in sick, leaving them short-staffed for the day. And then, with a great delighted smile, Candy broke the news that the emerald-cut pink that Jessica loved so much had been sold.

But the message that Ryan had already been in and left to attend a board meeting at the Pitt Street offices drained some of the unrelenting tension from her. Jessica gave a silent sigh of relief. At least she would have a while to prepare herself to face him again.

By midmorning, after a rush of customers, and several hours on her feet, Jessica needed a break. She made herself a cup of herb tea and retreated to her office to catch up with her latest batch of e-mails. That was where Ryan found her.

He entered her office, closed the door softly behind him and leaned against it. Jessica tensed, fearful of a confrontation after their last meeting, where she'd turned down his proposal before he'd even begun.

But she need not have worried.

"Hi. How are you feeling?" The eyes that scanned her held concern and something curiously like tenderness.

Jessica relaxed a little. "Tired. I'm gaining more weight than I should be."

He took a step forward and suddenly the space between the four walls seemed to shrink. "Can you feel the baby moving yet?"

"No, but my tummy is growing." Driven by the longing she read in his eyes, she said, "Do you want to feel?"

His face lit up. "I'll be gentle."

And Jessica felt a lump growing in her throat as he knelt before her and carefully put his hands on her belly.

"There is already a bit of a curve here," he said in surprise, his hand stroking her.

"I'm getting fat."

"You'll never be fat. You're gorgeous, Jess."

"Thank you." She beamed down at him. In a dark formal suit and old school tie he looked a little out of place on his knees. But he didn't seem to care. His large tanned hands were gentle on her body and Jessica could feel the caring in the tender touch of his fingers. Suddenly she didn't feel so tired, her body didn't feel so heavy. All because Ryan thought she was gorgeous, because he was touching her awkward belly with reverence.

"During my lunchtime I've got an appointment for my first

scan." She hesitated for a fraction of a second, then she plunged on. "Would you like to come?"

Ryan's eyes glowed with pleasure. "Wild horses wouldn't stop me."

And he was good at his word. In the doctor's reception, he held her hand tightly in his. When their time came to go in, Jessica introduced him to Dr. Waite and saw the doctor's eyes widen in recognition, before his surprise vanished and he bustled around while Jessica changed into a gown in a curtained cubicle.

"You can lie here," a nurse told her when she returned.

She lay down on the bed, wrinkling her nose at the smell of antiseptic, and Ryan sat in the chair beside her and took her hand again, while the nurse smeared her belly with a gel that was cool enough to make her gasp.

Seconds later Dr. Waite pointed at the screen. "See, there's the fetus."

Ryan's hand tightened around hers. "I can see it." His voice sounded hoarse, as though his throat, too, was burning with suppressed emotion.

Jessica peeped sideways at him. He sat hunched forward, staring at the monitor with an intensity he usually reserved for balance sheets.

"And, Jessica, here's the reason why you've been so tired and hungry. And the reason for your more than expected weight gain."

A pang of anxiety pierced Jessica. She stared at the blipping movement Dr. Waite had indicated. "What is it? What's wrong?"

"It's another beating heart."

"Another?" she said, bewildered, trying to make sense of the movement on the screen.

"Twins?" Ryan caught on quicker. "For Pete's sake, that's the last thing I ever expected."

Jessica flinched.

Not one baby. Twins. A ready-made family.

Ryan was going to regret that he'd ever started to propose to her and turn and run as far as his long, strong legs could take him. And she couldn't blame him one little bit. Why should he settle for a pregnant mechanic's daughter with twins on the way, when he could have his pick of Sydney's best-connected and most beautiful women?

"Are there twins in your family, Jessica? Fraternal twins can be hereditary on the mother's side," Dr. Waite was saying.

Her brain felt like it was made of warm wet noodles. She tried to concentrate. "My mother is a twin," she said slowly, still trying to come to terms with the shock, and thinking about the upheaval the discovery would cause her and Ryan.

But the look Ryan turned on her wasn't the look of a man about to run for his life. If Jessica hadn't known better, hadn't known how wary he was of losing the freedom of his bachelor/executive lifestyle, she might have been foolish enough to think that the glow in his eyes, the emotion she glimpsed there, might be love.

That evening, Ryan insisted on picking Jessica up from her apartment and taking her to dinner. "To celebrate," he told her firmly when she started to protest.

But it was more than that, he admitted to himself as he helped her into his car. He wasn't letting Jessica out of his sight. He wasn't giving her a chance to disappear, to take the joy out his life again.

He pulled in to the undercover parking ground and heard her breath catch.

"We're going to your penthouse? I thought we were going out."

"Don't worry. You won't need to cook." He gave her a wry smile. "I've arranged for Le Marquis to do takeout."

His comment had the desired effect. She gave a breathy laugh of surprise. "Le Marquis does takeout?"

"Well, not take out exactly." He cut the engine of the M6. "They've provided a chef to make it an authentic Le Marquis experience."

"A takeout chef? You shouldn't have gone to so much trouble." She turned wide brown eyes on him that held a hint of uncertainty in their depths.

"I thought rather than going out, you might want to relax," he said quietly. "So come upstairs, sit back, put your feet up and enjoy. No pressure."

"No pressure?"

"I'm not going to seduce you."

"Oh." Something like disappointment flitted across her expressive features.

Ryan refused to let himself think about what that non-committal little sound might mean as he went around and opened the passenger door for her. Tonight was not about sex.

Tonight was about Jessica.

To show her how special she was.

Upstairs in the living area the French doors onto the deck had been flung open to let in the warm summer evening. The gold of the setting sun cast a glow over the harbour beyond, while a French chef was setting the finishing touches to the first course, a masterly arrangement of iceberg lettuce, smoked salmon and dill. As they approached the table, he came forward and took Jessica's wrap with a flourish while Ryan pulled out her chair.

Once seated, the chef, who introduced himself as Pierre, rattled off the choices for the main course. Jessica selected sliced fillet of chicken with a creamy Roquefort sauce and Ryan chose Boeuf Bourguignon. Pierre made for the kitchen, leaving them alone.

For a couple of seconds silence hung between them. Then Jessica asked in a subdued voice, "How do you really feel about the babies?"

"Stunned. I've never thought of myself as a father." His whole identity had been built around being Howard Blackstone's only surviving son. "And certainly not as the father to twins."

Yet now both the prospect of marriage to Jessica and the idea of being a father to two flesh-and-blood miniatures of himself and Jessica intrigued him enough for him to want to convince Jessica that she *had* to marry him. Sooner rather than later. He didn't want to miss a moment of the roller-coaster experience.

"Are you furious?" she asked in that same low voice.

He stared at her in amazement. "Why should I be furious?"

"Because I fell pregnant?"

"It takes two." He gave her a wolfish grin, but she didn't smile back.

"You never thought I'd tried to trap you into marrying me?"

He tilted his head to one side. "Is that what's worrying you? You're thinking that I might be blaming you? That I might consider you did it deliberately?" He shook his head. "I don't."

Jessica let out a soft sigh, and Ryan's gaze sharpened. "What are you worrying about, Jess?"

"I'm not sure that you'll understand."

"Spit it out. We can work it out. Are you worried that the babies might sap everything out of you? That you're going to lose your identity? Don't be. If you want to work, we can arrange something. I know how important your career is to you."

She looked down. "It's strange. I always thought my job was everything to me. Then a couple of months ago something changed. Suddenly I realised I could walk away from

Blackstone's, from my career, and it wouldn't change who I was, what I believed."

"You mean when you discovered you were pregnant?"

"That was part of it." She met his gaze. "But not all of it. Remember we fought because I wanted us to spend Christmas together?"

He frowned. "Jess, we don't need to talk about past friction. Not tonight. Let's celebrate the baby...babies," he corrected himself.

She played with the napkin, unfolding it and balling it in her hand. "I *need* to tell you this. I wanted to spend that holiday with you because I needed reassurance from you that our relationship was heading somewhere."

He stretched his hand across the table and covered hers. "I'm sorry. I was selfish."

"But I didn't understand how important it was for you to spend time with your father at Byron Bay. Not back then. I felt hurt that you never invited me to share your family occasions. I thought you were ashamed of me."

"I was never ashamed of you. But I didn't want anyone knowing that I was having an affair with someone who worked for me." He'd lost Jessica because of his stupidity. "If I'm ashamed of anyone, it should be of myself. I should have been more considerate."

"I should've told you what I wanted." She dropped the napkin and threaded her fingers through his. "But I was torn apart. On the one hand, I was afraid of driving you away, that you would break off our relationship if I forced the issue— after all, I knew your stance. On the other hand, I wanted to force the issue. I wanted a commitment from you."

"Which I wasn't ready to give."

She glanced down, and her extravagantly long lashes covered her eyes. "Then I found out I was pregnant. It was a

shock. But I discovered I liked the idea of having a baby.
was ready for it. But you'd said—"

"No cats, no kids, no press, and certainly no diamon
rings!"

That got her attention. She stared at him, a little startled a
his self-deprecation. "Well, yes. So when the test stic
changed colour, I knew it was over."

"I wasn't ready for marriage," he admitted quietly. "I'n
so sorry, Jess."

"Okay, so I came back with this New Year's resolution t
end our relationship. I was going to be very staunch about it
I wasn't going to tell you about the baby until I'd come t
terms with it myself."

"But you didn't tell me."

Pressing her hands against her cheeks, she confessed
"Because I was angry with you for not giving me the com
mitment I wanted. I decided to fly straight to Auckland fo
the opening of the new jewellery store in the city. But I misse
my plane and I couldn't get another flight. I called Vina, Ric'
secretary, and she arranged for me to catch a ride with you
father on the chartered jet—even though normally I tried t
stay as far out his way as possible."

"Why?"

Jessica dropped her hands and looked away. "That's .
long story."

"I've got all night." Ryan had a feeling that whatever sh
had to tell him was important to their future together.

But Pierre chose that instant to emerge from the kitche
with their meals.

"Crème brûlée for dessert, *oui*?" Pierre asked, lookin;
from one to the other.

They both nodded.

When Pierre had vanished back into the kitchen and shu

he door again, Jessica picked up her knife and fork. For a few
ninutes they ate in silence, then she said, "My mother worked
or your father. First as a temp and later probably as what is
uphemistically called a 'travel escort' for years."

Ryan knew he should've been more surprised. But he
vasn't. Nor did he doubt what she was telling him. The pieces
itted. Her strange behaviour around his father had been
ension. It also explained why he'd vaguely remembered her
nother when he'd met her at the cemetery. He must've met
er in his father's office years ago.

"That's why you avoided my father, why you told me you
lespised him."

"Yes." Jessica drew a deep breath. "I once snooped in my
nother's things and read a note Howard had sent my mother.
t must've been after a scare that she might've fallen pregnant.
t scared me."

"What did it say?"

"That if she ever fell pregnant, she would have to get an
bortion."

Ryan paled. "Oh, my God."

If she was honest, that note had coloured her view of
Ryan, too. "Deep in my heart I thought you might expect the
ame of me."

"That's why you never told me about your pregnancy when
ou first found out." Now his skin was almost grey, and he
poked haggard. "I would *never* have asked that of you. I can
ardly believe that he expected that of your mother."

She breathed a deep sigh of thanks. Ryan was nothing
ke his father. "I'm sorry I doubted you. And, Ryan, I know
e's your father, that you say he loved your mother and
nourned your brother's disappearance. I know that you
dmire him. But I never saw that side of him. I only saw
ne ruthless businessman and the womaniser. I was terrified

that my mother's affair with him would break up m
parents' marriage."

He chewed and swallowed, barely tasting the last mouthful
of the fine meal. "I can understand that. It must have been ver
difficult for you to become my lover with all that baggage."

She gave him a small smile. "The day at Miramare, yo
said that you didn't seem capable of resisting me." Her smil
widened. "Well, it's mutual. What chance did I have? Yo
were gorgeous, clever and you could charm birds out of trees
I tried very hard not to fall for you, but how could I resist?"

Colour stained the slash of his cheekbones. "You exagger
ate." A moment later he asked, "Was that what you argued abou
with my father in the airport? His treatment of your mother?"

"No." Her gaze held his. "We argued about you."

About him? Given her relationship with his father, it coul
not have been good. "Tell me, Jess."

"He'd found out about…us. That we were having an affai
that I was living in your apartment."

Ryan sat back. His father must have used a detective. Tha
too, would not surprise him. "And?"

"He wanted me to break it off with you. He told me
wasn't fit to be a Blackstone consort. An escort maybe,
consort never. 'Like mother, like daughter' were his exac
words."

Ryan bit back a stream of curses. They wouldn't wipe th
grief out of Jessica's eyes. The pain that his own flesh an
blood had put there.

"He only reinforced that I would never be good enough fo
you, that I would always be the mistress's daughter."

"Bollocks," Ryan said. "No one thinks of you as that. M
sister admires you, so does Ric. And Dani likes you, too. Peopl
respect you for the smart, clever woman you are. Don't let m
father strip you of your confidence. He was a master of that.

"That wasn't all." Her mouth barely moved and her lips were pale.

Ryan had to crane his neck to hear her. Again he felt a stab of anger that his father could've hurt her so much. "I want to know every detail, however minor you might consider it."

"We boarded the jet, then he threatened me. He told me that if I refused to break it off with you, he would fire me and disinherit you." Jessica's eyes were dark with remembered pain. "But if I did what he wanted, I'd get to keep my job *and* he'd consider not leaving all his shares to his eldest child. I thought he meant Kimberley. It never occurred to me that he might be speaking about James."

"What did you say?" Ryan's voice was rough with fury.

"I'd already decided to break it off with you so I told him that I quit and I walked off the jet."

"Good for you." But already he was trying to make sense of this new revelation. Jessica had never told him she'd quit.

"I was furious and upset. And on my way out, I nearly ran down Marise boarding the jet. I was way too uptight to go to the penthouse. I knew I was going to have to see you to tell you it was all over, and I wanted to think it all out. I'd quit, so I couldn't go back to work the next morning—everyone thought I was in Auckland."

"So where did you go?"

"It was getting late, so I went to my apartment. I knew I would be moving back soon. I ended up spending the night here. I figured that you would think I was already in Auckland, so I had a day's grace."

"After the jet went missing in the dark hours of the following morning, a passenger list was faxed through that still had your name on it. I nearly died myself." It had been the worst moment of his life. Coming on top of the shock that his father was missing, too, he'd gone wild with grief. "I tried to call you in the vain hope that you'd caught another carrier. Bu you weren't answering." He'd thought she was dead. He' been distraught. And then guilt had kicked in because he wa less concerned about his father than his lover. He'd throw himself into tracking the search-and-rescue operation and th funeral preparations. Anything to avoid the alarming susp cion that he might be vulnerable to an emotion he'd neve sought.

"My cell phone was off," she explained. "I didn't want speak to you. Not until I'd decided what I was going to say end it. Then it was too late. I heard on the news that your father plane had gone missing. So I went to your penthouse. I though you might need me." Jessica looked shattered. "Why didn't yo ever tell me all this? That you thought I'd died?"

Ryan shook his head. "I got back to the town house, afte an appalling day, to find you watching the news of my father disappearance on TV. There was so much to be done, I ha to stay focused, do what needed to be done. There would b enough time to come to terms with the emptiness later There'd been a treacherous moment when he'd wondere what she'd been doing booked to travel on his father's cha tered jet…and why she'd kept quiet about it. It had been horrible suspicion that had lasted only for a fraction of second and he'd thrust it out of his mind until Kitty Lang ha stirred it all up again.

Something in his expression must have alerted Jessica his thoughts. "That's when the suspicion began that ther was something going on between Howard and me," she sai slowly with a sense of dawning realisation.

"It didn't help that you grew increasingly pale and with drawn over the past month." His mouth kinked. "That did littl to reassure me."

Jessica pushed her plate aside. "I was unhappy…an

pregnant. I needed to end our relationship, but you were hurting. How could I be so unfeeling as to walk out during a time of such grief?"

"And I didn't make it any easier for you." He'd been so focused on the search-and-rescue effort last month, and this month his attention had been concentrated on the fallout from the will, compounded by his puerile resentment of Ric and the blazing animosity from Matt Hammond. Yet, startlingly, somewhere in the past couple of days since discovering that Jessica was pregnant, he'd discovered that he *did* want to get married. Nothing would make him happier than a future with Jessica and their children.

He loved Jessica. The discovery hadn't hit him suddenly. Instead it had sneaked up on him gradually, like the silvery early-morning mists that sometimes crept up from the sea over the beach house at Byron Bay.

It had taken him a while to realize that what he felt for her was love. Partially because he'd been so resistant to the idea of committing to a woman and giving up his independence. But mostly because he hadn't been able to see beyond the incredibly fierce passion she aroused in him, to the tender emotion that lay beyond.

He wanted Jessica to share the rest of his life.

As his wife.

Yet he could hardly blame her for refusing him. She'd lived with him, and he'd never attempted to make her more than a mistress, unknowingly echoing his father's treatment of her mother. How could he blame her for thinking that he was no better than his father? How could he ever convince her how much he needed her?

He stretched out a hand. "Jessica—"

"Dessert is splendid." Pierre burst from the kitchen. He set the ramekins down and kissed his fingertips. "Splendid."

Ryan drew back his hand, suppressing his urge to reach for Jessica, hold her and protect her from anything that might harm her.

"Thank you, Pierre."

"I have brewed the coffee. It is in the kitchen with two cups. Now it is time for me to go, *oui?*"

"*Oui,*" Ryan agreed, giving the chef a man-to-man look. And, in a magically short time, Pierre had packed up his utensils and tiptoed into the elevator, leaving Ryan alone with Jessica.

Ten

After Pierre had left, they finished the rich creamy desserts before making their way to the living area. Jessica plopped herself down, kicked her sandals off and wriggled her toes.

"Feet sore?" Ryan asked.

"Not really."

He lifted them and propped them on the arm of the sofa. "Lie back, relax."

"Right now I feel replete." She closed her eyes with a contented sigh until, unable to bear the silence that had fallen, her lashes fluttered upward to see what Ryan was doing. He stood beside her, staring down at her with an odd expression.

"What are you thinking?" she probed.

He hesitated.

"Tell me," she demanded.

"I'm thinking of all the mornings I've woken and watched you sleeping in my bed. The crescent shadows your lashes form on your skin, how you always kick your legs free of the covers, the way you sleep with your hand under your cheek."

She blinked. "You've studied me sleeping?"

"Often."

And she'd thought he barely noticed her, took her for granted. "Why?"

"You always look so at peace when you sleep, so beautiful. It gave me sense of pleasure. Something to carry with me all day long."

"I never knew." Strangely she didn't feel freaked out by the fact that he'd watched her sleep without her knowledge. The idea that he'd carried that memory with him every day was flattering.

"I've missed those minutes each morning." His jade eyes darkened.

Jessica stilled, barely daring to breathe as she absorbed his revelations. "I never knew. Although I remember sometimes waking to the sound of the door closing when you left in the morning." And feeling desperately alone.

"It was tough to leave without kissing you goodbye."

She gave him a glance from under her lashes. No humour glinted in his eyes. He was perfectly serious. "You should've kissed me."

"You looked so at peace, I didn't want to waken you."

"Well, you can make up for it by kissing me now."

He bent his head. His lips were gentle on hers, his breath warm. Her pulse quickened as it always did when he came near. His hand caressed her shoulder, drawing her toward him and deepening the kiss.

Jessica felt emotion surge deep within her heart. So strong. And so sweet. As his tongue pressed into her mouth, Ryan's hand stroked along her throat, down between her breasts… and stopped on her belly.

It lay there, motionless.

A frisson of expectation swept her.

He broke the kiss and lifted his head. "You're wearing too many clothes."

"Maybe I am."

"This time I'm taking them off." The look he gave her was hot enough to singe. "You're not hiding anything from me. And this time, not only do I look, I get to touch, too."

Before she could murmur a protest, he swung her up into his arms and carried her up the stairs, his breathing barely growing heavier. By the time he set her down carefully on the wide king-size bed, Jessica had lost any desire to object.

Her heart pounded as he knelt on the covers beside her, his shoulders broad under a white cotton shirt.

In the light of the bedside lamp, his face was all angles. The shadows gave his expression a sensual intensity, a passionate power that caught at her throat and increased her heartbeat to a drumroll.

Her skirt came off in one sweep of his hand; the silver top took only a moment more and he dealt with her lacy bra and briefs with the same ruthless efficiency.

Jessica felt a brief flare of self-consciousness as she lay naked across the covers, while he loomed over her still fully clothed, until his head tilted so that the lamplight fell directly across his face and she read the expression in his eyes.

Sensation rushed through her. Warm. Supple. Like honey melting in the sun. So very sweet. And making her feel all woman.

"I've been a fool." He said it so softly, she barely heard. "The greatest jewel of all lay in my possession all the time. I nearly lost it."

"Oh, Ryan."

"I love you, Jess."

The poignant openness in his usually closed expression revealed the truth. He loved her!

"I'm sorry I never realised what you meant…what you were worth to me. I'll make it up to you, I promise. If you'll let me."

Let him? As if she'd be fool enough to turn him away.…

"All I ever wanted from you was your love." She opened her arms wide.

And then he was shucking off his clothes. As always, Jessica couldn't stop admiring the sheer beauty of his nude body. His hips were lean and his flanks smooth. He came down on the bed beside her, his stomach muscles rippling in the lamplight, the light dusting of hair tapering down to where his erection jutted out, revealing how much he desired her.

But when he touched her, the ravenous hunger she'd anticipated was tempered and his hands were tender. On her face, her breasts, her stomach.

His lips followed the trail his fingers had carved out. He pressed his lips against the rise of her belly. "Mine."

She smiled at the possessive declaration. "There'll be much more there in the months to come."

"I'll relish every moment." His eyes glinted. "I like your curves…your lush breasts…the voluptuousness. Very sexy. I can't believe I didn't realise you were pregnant sooner."

"I can. You've had a lot on your mind."

"Not so much that you shouldn't have been at the forefront. But I swear I'll make it up to you." His hand stroked lower.

Jessica gasped as his fingers touched the soft, wet core of her. Her body shivered as his touch became more insistent, sensation shafted through her. "Oh, goodness!"

His fingers moved more slickly as the heat of her body lubricated his hand.

Ripples raged through her in widening rings, consuming her. She arched her back and moaned out loud.

Instantly Ryan shifted himself over her, propping himself n his elbows, holding his weight off her, and Jessica went quid at the caring in his eyes.

When he sank into her, it felt different from ever before. he white-hot passion was still there, bubbling through her loodstream. But as the ripples started all over again, she felt ven more. A warmth, a feeling of being cherished and pro- ected. Of being special beyond price.

Afterwards he couldn't keep his hands off her. He stroked er hair off her face, stroked her breasts, and, as if drawn by compulsion stronger than he could control, he touched her tomach again. "I still can't believe it."

Jessica raised her head. The eyes that met hers held a heart- topping tenderness. Her breath caught.

Disbelief shot through her. "You're pleased about the babies!"

The smile that curved his mouth was more than a little heepish. "And proud. I can't wait to tell the whole world that ou're pregnant."

Tell everyone? Ryan wanted the world to know that she vas pregnant? She had never expected that. "Wait a mo- nent…"

"You will marry me, won't you, Jess?" Concern flitted hrough his glorious green eyes before he suppressed it.

Jessica could barely assimilate it all. He said he loved her. Ie still wanted to marry her. The delight and joy was back tronger than before.

"Don't answer now. Think about it. I'll give you until the ight of the jewellery showing to absorb it." This time his mile was slow and sure.

The rest of the days leading up to the launch of the Some- hing Old, Something New collection flashed past in a mad ush. On Friday afternoon, Jessica stood back to find that ev-

erything had somehow miraculously come together. All th
details were under control and there was nothing left for her t
do.

Confident that everything was running smoothly for th
evening to come, Jessica left to have a manicure and her hai
done. Then she returned to her apartment to take a coc
shower to rid herself of the afternoon heat.

Once showered, Jessica dressed in a summery creatio
the colour of watermelon and embroidered with fine, clea
beads that gave an added shimmer. The dress had a dee
halter neckline and a fitted top that showed off her lush, newl
acquired cleavage, and the full skirt swirled around her legs

Staring into the mirror, Jessica knew that tonight no on
could doubt that she was pregnant. There was a fullness t
her breasts, a ripeness to the curve of her stomach that th
bodice couldn't possibly hide, unlike the flowing tops she'
been wearing to work.

She couldn't help wondering what Ryan was doing, wha
he'd be wearing tonight.

When the doorbell rang, Jessica frowned, tempted t
ignore it. A cab was coming to pick her up. If she dallied sh
would be late. The bell rang again. She wrenched the doc
open and her mouth went dry.

Ryan stood there in a black tuxedo, looking utterly devas
tating.

"What are you doing here?"

"I've come to take you to the event of the year."

"I thought I was meeting you there."

"So did I. But then I realised you have to go with me."

Curiosity got the better of her. "Why?"

"So that by tomorrow no one in Sydney will have an
doubt of how I feel about you." Ryan rocked back on hi
heels. "You've always intimated that I hide you away. I'v

vowed that you'll never again be my secret mistress. After tonight there will be no doubt exactly what our relationship is and how much you mean to me. Now finish getting ready and let's go."

Jessica quickly fastened her pearls around her neck, clasped a thick gold bangle around her wrist and slid into a pair of silver sandals. A light spray of perfume, a final application of lipgloss and she was ready to go.

She and Ryan were among the first to arrive. Jessica slipped upstairs to check that the models, stylists and jewellery designers were all there among the organized chaos. Satisfied that everything was running as smoothly as could be expected, she returned downstairs to Ryan's side.

The space had filled up with Sydney's glamorous, A-list crowd. Some were already seated and were chatting among themselves. A T-ramp carpeted in crimson had been erected at the bottom of the stairs that led to the floor where the showroom was situated. Overhead the chandeliers glittered and light scintillated off the jewels worn by the guests. Waiters circulated with trays loaded with glasses of champagne, cosmopolitans and an assortment of hors d'oeuvres.

"It's going to be a full house." Jessica tipped her head up to Ryan. "Everything looks wonderful."

"It certainly does." Ryan gave her a slow smile.

Jessica felt herself flush at the concentration of his attention on her. "I meant, all your planning and hard work is paying off."

"Your hard work, too," he said. "And don't forget all the other people who played a part. It's been a team effort."

"Jessica...Ryan." Briana's gaze was very interested as she took in how close Ryan stood to Jessica.

Jessica turned and gave her friend a hug. "Are you all ready?"

"I'm about to go and do a lightning-fast change into what

I'll be modelling first. I shouldn't even be down here. I just wanted to make sure Jake didn't feel lost."

"Jake Vance?" Jessica started to smile. "He's here with you tonight?"

Briana shook her head. "I told you, Jess, it's not serious." And then she was gone.

Ryan led Jessica to the front row where seats had been reserved for them. A little distance back Jessica caught a glimpse of Dani Hammond, elegantly clad in a sleek black dress, her curls fiercely pulled back from a face pale with nerves, the severity of the style broken by a spray of twinkling gems in her hair. Beside her sat her mother, Sonya, elegant and restrained. Jessica gave them both a quick wave and again watched the quickly masked astonishment as they took in Ryan hovering beside her.

Jessica suppressed a smile. Ryan had been right. By the end of the night everyone would know what the relationship between Ryan Blackstone and his store manager was.

When Ryan got up onto the red carpet, the capacity crowd stilled. On the large screen that formed a backdrop, pictures flashed as he spoke. Of Janderra. Of fancy-hued diamonds. Of the designers involved in the collections being launched tonight.

An image of the Desert Star flashed up, the first significant diamond find at Janderra. Ryan spoke of the wealth of talent that Blackstone's Jewellery had developed; he introduced the designers and welcomed Dani Hammond as the newest star. Jessica glanced across to see his cousin blushing furiously, while Sonya smiled proudly.

Then Jessica heard her name, saw a picture of herself flash up as Ryan introduced her as the hard-working manager of the Sydney store. Her cheeks went hot. Now how was she ever going to be able to resign? Perhaps they could work out something that allowed her shorter hours in the store after the birth of the twins.

When he'd finished, one of Australia's favourite female pop icons appeared at the top of the stairs and sashayed down singing the seventies hit "Diamonds Are Forever," her voice pure and true. She was closely followed by Briana wearing a fabulous ballgown and a collar of dazzling diamonds. On the giant screen a close-up of the collar made the crowd gasp.

The show had begun. The newest series of famed Blackstone's collections had arrived.

"Who's that?" Jessica leaned toward Ryan and he bent his head to catch her whisper. As promised, he stood at her side, his hand possessively wrapped around her waist, making it clear to everyone that she was with him.

"Who?"

"That tall, very handsome, dark-haired stranger who has been staring at Briana like he's been hit by lightning. The one whom one or two of the newshounds seem to be sniffing around with keen interest."

Ryan followed her gaze and started to frown. "That's Jarrod Hammond. And the reporters are fascinated by a Hammond turning up. They're waiting to see if there will be any more scandal tonight."

"That's Jarrod Hammond?" Jessica looked at him curiously. "Funny, he doesn't look at all like what I expected. He's quite different from Matt, although I have to admit I only caught the briefest glimpse of Matt at the funeral."

"They're not related by birth. My Aunt Katherine and Uncle Oliver weren't able to have any children. That's why it was such a bitter blow when old granddad Jeb gave the Heart of the Outback to my mother when James was born."

Jessica studied the features of the man who appeared to be

oblivious to everyone in the room except for Briana. "So Jarrod Hammond is adopted?"

"Yep. But he was still brought up a Hammond, so warn Briana to watch every move he makes," Ryan growled darkly.

A tall, very slim model was showing off a pair of spectacular diamond-drop earrings to oohs and aahs from the crowd.

As each new model came on, the pieces became more and more spectacular. "Judging from the appreciative sounds, I'd say that the launch is a runaway success," Ryan said softly in her ear.

She nodded. "I think you're right."

"Well done. A large part of this is because of you."

Ryan was proud of her, pleased with the success of the launch, and for the first time Jessica realized that Ryan viewed her as his equal. She was more than a match for him.

The music started to build. "The finale is coming."

And then Briana was coming down the stairs, wearing an exquisitely simple wedding dress that left her shoulders bare and fell around her feet in soft folds. Behind her walked three models dressed as bridesmaids, their hair braided into plaits and wound around their heads, diamonds dripping from their arms, which held baskets filled with white roses.

By contrast Briana's hair hung loose and she wore a crown of white rosebuds. Around her neck glittered a single suspended pendant.

"The Desert Star," someone gasped beside them. Applause thundered through the room.

"Look at Jarrod Hammond's expression," Jessica whispered to Ryan. "He's a goner."

"Not if Briana has any sense. He's a Hammond."

"Oh, Ryan! You never change."

"You know, I think I am changing," he murmured enigmatically. "It won't be easy for Jarrod. Don't forget who his brother is and who Briana's sister was."

"Oh, good grief. Matt and Marise."

"I wouldn't bet on Jarrod managing to surmount those obstacles."

"Then it's just as well I don't bet," said Jessica primly.

Ryan laughed out loud, pulled her closer to his side and dropped a kiss on her hair.

"Hush," she said, "it's the big moment."

He turned his head to see that Briana and her bridesmaids had arrayed themselves along the ramp and started to toss the long-stemmed white roses into the audience. One landed in Ryan's hands and, with a flourish, he handed it to Jessica.

"For you."

She took it from him, flushing with pleasure.

With the departure of the bride and her attendants, the show came to an end. Ric Perrini spoke a few words in closing. The crowd rose to their feet for a moment of silence in memory of Howard Blackstone and all who had died aboard the jet with him.

Ryan shut his eyes and felt each second pass in time to his heartbeat. *Goodbye, Dad. Rest in peace.* He felt an unexpected and appalling sense of loss. His father was gone, forever.

But Jessica had been spared.

His love was alive. He pulled her into his arms, heard her soft gasp and tightened his arms around her, oblivious to the stares they were attracting.

He bent his head, so that his mouth was beside her ear. "You know, the worst hours of my life were when I thought you'd died in that crash with my father." He brushed a tender kiss against her temple, uncaring of what anyone thought. "I have changed. I will never be like my father."

He put a finger under her chin and tipped it up so he could

look down into her delicate features. "I love you, Jess. Please marry me."

"Even though it will mean the end of your executive bachelor status?" Joy danced in her eyes. "Even though you'll have a wife and two children before the year is out?"

"That's not going to scare me off."

"Is this the same man who always vowed, 'No cats, no kids, no press, no diamond rings'?"

"Hey, that started crumbling a while ago. I told you, as long as you come back, I don't mind if you bring that damn cat with you."

"His name is Picasso."

"Right. And I already asked you to marry me *after* you told me about the baby. So there goes *no kids*."

"That was when there was only one baby under discussion, there are now two. I won't blame you if you head for the hills."

"I won't be heading for the hills." He wound his arms around her. "I won't be going anywhere far from you. The *no press* thing was already blown out the water after the races at Flemington."

"I didn't realise you'd seen that photo in the paper."

"How could I miss it?" He pulled a face at her. "My sister thrust it under my nose the moment I set foot on the jet that morning. She thinks you're good for me."

"Oh," said Jessica, lost for words.

"The only one left on the list is the diamond ring. And I've already tried to give it to you, but you refused to let me."

Jessica caught her breath. She grabbed Ryan's hand and placed it on stomach with trembling hands. "I don't think I'm going to be allowed to refuse this time round."

"What was that?"

Her powerful corporate warrior sounded utterly terrified.

"I think one of our babies just decided to rock our world."

"Wow." Under their hands one of the babies moved again, a tiny flutter of life. Ryan's eyes lit up with wonder.

And in that moment, Jessica realised that Ryan wanted them all, her and her babies. The whole ready-made family.

"Yes, I'll marry you."

"Because of the babies?" His smile was wry.

"No, because I love you."

The ring box he took from his pocket showed no sign of being soaked in the swimming pool. But when he flipped it open, Jessica's breath left her lungs. "You remembered."

She stared at the ring she'd spent the months admiring, talking people out of buying. "Candy told me it had been sold. I was so disappointed. I thought that was a sign that marriage and me were not meant to be."

Ryan laughed. Before she could say another word he slipped the ring on her finger and stopped a passing waiter to snag two glasses of mineral water from the tray.

"To us."

"To us."

They stared at each other in wonder.

Somewhere behind her, Dani gave a shriek. "Jessica, lift up your hand! Is that an engagement ring? Ryan, you sneaky thing, no one even knew!"

Champagne corks started to pop. Everyone crowded around, giving congratulations. Kimberley and Ric. Briana with Jake. Vincent and the rest of the Blackstone cousins. As well as Sonya and Garth, who were a little more restrained in their delight. Then everyone raised their glasses and toasted, "To Ryan and Jessica."

"You do realise we'll have to contact a Realtor. I'm going to need to put the penthouse on the market," he murmured in her ear when the hullabaloo had subsided. "I have it on good authority it's not the kind of place where twins can leave sticky fingers."

A flash of blonde ringlets and the dangle of gold earrings across the room caused Jessica to whisper, "I know she's a top-notch Realtor, but we're not retaining Kitty Lang."

"Earlier Kitty looked like she's snaring herself a rich man. She may not be available." Ryan grinned. "All I care about is finding a house where you and the kids can be happy."

"And the cat. Don't forget about Picasso." Jessica peered at him from under her eyelashes as he threw his head back and laughed out loud. "And, of course, you need to be happy, too."

Ryan bent toward her, "I'll be a happy man—and our house will be filled with the sound of laughter—as long as I have you by my side." And then his mouth closed over hers in a loving kiss.

* * * * *

DIAMONDS DOWN UNDER
continues next month with Maxine Sullivan's
MISTRESS & A MILLION DOLLARS—
only in Silhouette Desire!

Silhouette®

Desire

Buy 2 Silhouette Desire books and receive

$1.00 off

your purchase of the Silhouette Desire novel
Iron Cowboy by *New York Times* bestselling author

DIANA PALMER

on sale March 2008.

Receive $1.00 off

**the Silhouette Desire novel IRON COWBOY,
on sale March 2008, when you purchase
2 Silhouette Desire books.**

*Available wherever books are sold including most bookstores,
supermarkets, drugstores and discount stores.*

Coupon expires August 31, 2008. Redeemable at participating retail
outlets in the U.S. only. Limit one coupon per customer.

5 65373 00076 2   (8100) 0 11470

SDCPNUS0208

Silhouette® Desire

Buy 2 Silhouette Desire books and receive

$1.⁰⁰ off

your purchase of the Silhouette Desire novel
Iron Cowboy by *New York Times* bestselling author

DIANA PALMER

on sale March 2008.

Receive $1.⁰⁰ off

**the Silhouette Desire novel IRON COWBOY,
on sale March 2008, when you purchase
2 Silhouette Desire books.**

*Available wherever books are sold including most bookstores,
supermarkets, drugstores and discount stores.*

Coupon expires August 31, 2008. Redeemable at participating retail
outlets in Canada only. Limit one coupon per customer.

52608214

SDCPNCAN0208

REQUEST YOUR FREE BOOKS!

2 FREE NOVELS PLUS 2 FREE GIFTS!

Silhouette® Desire®

Passionate, Powerful, Provocative!

YES! Please send me 2 FREE Silhouette Desire® novels and my 2 FREE gifts. After receiving them, if I don't wish to receive any more books, I can return the shipping statement marked "cancel." If I don't cancel, I will receive 6 brand-new novels every month and be billed just $3.80 per book in the U.S., or $4.47 per book in Canada, plus 25¢ shipping and handling per book and applicable taxes, if any*. That's a savings of almost 15% off the cover price! I understand that accepting the 2 free books and gifts places me under no obligation to buy anything. I can always return a shipment and cancel at any time. Even if I never buy another book from Silhouette, the two free books and gifts are mine to keep forever.

225 SDN EEXJ 326 SDN EEXU

Name	(PLEASE PRINT)	
Address		Apt.
City	State/Prov.	Zip/Postal Code

Signature (if under 18, a parent or guardian must sign)

Mail to the **Silhouette Reader Service™:**
IN U.S.A.: P.O. Box 1867, Buffalo, NY 14240-1867
IN CANADA: P.O. Box 609, Fort Erie, Ontario L2A 5X3

Not valid to current Silhouette Desire subscribers.

Want to try two free books from another line?
Call 1-800-873-8635 or visit www.morefreebooks.com.

* Terms and prices subject to change without notice. NY residents add applicable sales tax. Canadian residents will be charged applicable provincial taxes and GST. This offer is limited to one order per household. All orders subject to approval. Credit or debit balances in a customer's account(s) may be offset by any other outstanding balance owed by or to the customer. Please allow 4 to 6 weeks for delivery.

Your Privacy: Silhouette is committed to protecting your privacy. Our Privacy Policy is available online at www.eHarlequin.com or upon request from the Reader Service. From time to time we make our lists of customers available to reputable firms who may have a product or service of interest to you. If you would prefer we not share your name and address, please check here. ☐

SDES07